Night Walking

by

Bo Noir

Gueraville Books

I0571177

Copyright © 2014 by Gueraville Books

All rights reserved.

This is a work of fiction. Names, characters, businesses, places, events and incidents are either the products of the author's imagination or used in a fictitious manner. Any resemblance to actual persons, living or dead, or actual events is purely coincidental.

ISBN: 978-0-9904848-1-3

Editing by MRBP

Cover Design by Jeffrey Cajucom

Cover Illustration by Sophia Michailidou

For my little family, K and F

You have my love always

Chapter 1

It was a cool and beautiful Sunday morning, and the kind people of the suburban pasture were busily taking care of weekend chores and reacquainting themselves with neighbors over picket fences. There were well-groomed kids running around the lawns, playing with the sprinklers as if they were dancing in the rain. This neighborhood was a pure catalog of Kodak moments. And caught in the middle of the photograph was little old Beebee.

Beebee was a small, white, fluffy Pomeranian-mix dog. Lying on the grass, she looked around her yard with mixed emotions. Her intelligence was above average for a dog, and her face suggested a pensive disposition. While there was warm sun on her face and plenty of water and treats to munch, there was something missing. Absent from all the other yards were other curious pooches. By chance, all the other houses were full of cat people. And those cat people owned plenty of indoor cats. There were only a couple of outdoor cats, and they didn't come around, as if they regarded Beebee's backyard beneath them. Beebee only saw other dogs occasionally when she would go to the veterinarian. Even in that stressful environment, she squeezed in every bit of coquettish playtime while in the waiting room with the other sick canines. In her dog brain her thoughts were clear, though no human could understand them. "wow. much lonesomeness. such desolation," she pondered.

The paperboy rolled along the street and threw Sunday's heavy issue over the fence, unnecessarily emphasizing his surprisingly bad aim, sending the paper to land on top of Beebee's head. Smack! The dog barked angrily at the paperboy, who sped away as soon as he heard the dog yelp. Beebee kept barking, mostly out of spite. She wondered why she even lay down in exactly the same spot every day, just to get hit by the pitiful paperboy. Without friends, it was the only thing to do around here.

Beebee was the "practice baby" for Gladys and her oaf of a husband Roy. Once married and in love, they had planned a family perfect for Town and Country magazine. They'd gotten Beebee to see how they would do taking care of a living thing more complicated than an air plant. This would give them an idea of what they would be like as parents. It certainly did. Beebee's presence brought out the truth that Roy would be a lousy and indifferent father. Beebee also summoned the truth about Gladys. She would be a wonderful and attentive mother who would shower the babies with unconditional love.

Roy's shortcomings didn't stop them from trying to have kids. After all, that was the fun part. They tried and tried again, but nothing happened.

Then they spent thousands on counseling and fertility treatments. And eventually they accepted that a biological union of their two souls would never happen. The practice baby became the surrogate baby for Gladys, and the clump of fur on which to wipe chip-greased hands for Roy.

Roy had been a handsome man once. Tall and athletic, he had been captain of the rugby team in college. He had arms like tree trunks and a ridiculously low percentage of body fat. Seeing him for the first time, any woman would have pushed her boyfriend into an icy river. Though he retained his bulk, his body fat percent continued to rise with inflation. And his hairline rose northward, with every indication that when it reached the pinnacle of his dome, it would keep on going and recede southward behind his head. The shabbiest part of him wasn't related to his body, but to his mind. Every day after work, he would come home and plop his butt onto the couch. And he would never bring Gladys home a gift after his various business trips. Never lifting a finger to help Gladys around the house, he just added to the chores for her to do. This decline and coldness had begun years ago, and showed no sign of lifting.

Looking out the window, Gladys looked at her pretty white Beebee moping on the grass. This won't do, Gladys thought, and grimly stormed out of the kitchen into the living room where her husband sat engrossed by the TV.

In her younger years, she had clipped photos of houses from lifestyle magazines, carefully planning the house she wanted to have eighteen years in advance. But shortly after marrying Roy, she'd accepted the fact that it was never a realistic prospect to begin with. She looked around the living room and daydreamed for a split second about what it could've looked like if things hadn't gone so wrong. She was pulled back into reality by Beebee's sad eyes. Gladys groaned in frustration.

"Did you take Beebee for a walk? Just wondering, as that was your only chore for the day!" Gladys asked Roy as she stood by the doorway. She already knew Roy hadn't walked Beebee yet. She felt a pang of pity for Beebee, who was also stuck around the house with lazy Roy. Out of habit and desperation, she still hoped he would remember, and get off the goddamn couch and take the task off her hands. But Roy kept watching TV, his eyes glued to the screen, his feet littered with empty cans of beer Gladys would be cleaning up later. "So?" Gladys asked, louder this time, when she realized Roy wasn't paying attention to her. He was very good at practicing selective hearing, which Gladys envied just a tad.

"Hmm? What was that, honey?" Roy muttered, not even bothering to look at Gladys as he fumbled around the low table by the side of the couch in search of another can of beer. He found one, took a sip, and was disappointed that it was empty.

"I'm talking about this living creature that we have responsibility for. The furry one at my feet. Who, I may add, was your idea to get. You said you were going to walk her today!" Gladys explained, moving closer to the couch so she could emphasize the point. Beebee cooperated in this scolding and tugged on Roy's pant-leg with her teeth.

"Honey, the game is on!" Roy said, as if it were an explanation for everything. Moronically, he took another sip of beer from the empty can, forgetting that it was empty. "Hey, if you're going to take her out for a walk, can you run by the store and get me some more beer?" Roy implored, finally facing her with the goofy smile that used to give her butterflies. Now, Gladys saw it simply as the symbol of Roy's unbelievable indifference and self-centeredness.

"This is my only day off! Fucking beer!" Gladys said, not really worried that Roy would hear. He would hear, Gladys thought dimly, but he wouldn't have enough brain cells to interpret it. She stormed out of the living room, stopped by the front door to step into her boots, and opened the door to leave. Then a thought occurred to her, and she had to vocalize. "Yeah, maybe I'll walk her all the way to Ireland and get you the freshest Guinness in the world, my dear! Hopefully it takes me the rest of my life. Maybe I'll pass the husband store on the way!" Gladys added. It was such wishful thinking.

"Hmm? Yeah, you're the best, babe!" Roy yelled, paying her no attention as usual. Then he was back to browsing through the channels for other sports games, since the one he'd been watching had already ended. You could get off that chair and walk Beebee and get your fucking beer now since the game is no longer on, Gladys thought in frustration, but didn't bother to voice it out loud anymore. It was very tiring to talk to Roy, seeing how her husband had turned into some sort of imbecile. Gladys stormed out of the house with Beebee in tow. The two neglected ladies moved on down the street, stomping churlishly as they went.

This particular Sunday morning, Gladys chose her favorite outfit, which was comprised of white Keds, blue jeans and a red button top. Cool, crisp and classic, she thought. The look played well against her alabaster skin and ginger red hair. It was not fancy, but she didn't care. It was the best she could do, since her job had been cut back and she only worked part time. Though she had lived in the neighborhood for a long time, she was sometimes mistaken for an au pair to a wealthy couple. She was 35 but looked half that age. Some people don't wrinkle much, but Gladys was in the top 1% of smooth-faced thirty-somethings. Her figure had not changed that much from her roaring twenties, either. She still filled out her jeans with enough arcs and roundabouts that the errant BMW would occasionally slow down as it passed her by, so that the banker pervert inside could ogle her juicy behind for just a second longer. Her frontage was substantial, too. It was as if someone had taken the Sidney opera house and placed it on her chest. She had developed late in life, after being pretty flat-chested for most of her teens. When her ample boobage started to emerge, Mother Nature had forgotten to install an off switch, because the breasts kept growing until they were more of a pain in the ass and lower back than anything else. She had put on a few pounds since her younger years, but was so skinny to begin with that she looked quite healthy and normal now.

Gladys strolled Beebee around as her neighbors went on with their weekend lawn mowing. Some kids were playing hockey in the street. Then, along the opposite side of the street, coming towards Gladys, was a mom train. A mom train is a sequence of at least three mothers pushing baby carriages in tandem. It was depressing enough to see families spending quality time with each other, but the sight of new mothers really struck a chord in her heart. This time it was four mothers with strollers, one right after the other. They rolled past Gladys and paid her no mind as she politely pulled Beebee to the side of the curb. Gladys felt a mixture of sadness and a little regret. She rubbed her palm flat against her stomach and held her head down. She brushed the sad thoughts off quickly and focused her attention on Beebee.

"Beebee, it's just you and me, kid," Gladys whispered to the fur ball as she rubbed her behind the ears. Beebee just barked in response, but thought "such pair. much solidarity." Gladys let out a sigh of defeat, hugging the pitiful Beebee, who just wanted to get the walk over with.

"Sad thing is, that is the smartest thing I've heard all weekend," Gladys murmured, as she cuddled with Beebee. "The noises your daddy makes are far more primitive," Gladys added subconsciously, taking her back to the ugly mental place. "Ugh! Come on!"

Leaving that outdoor museum of perfect lives behind, they walked to the entrance of their local woods. Once inside they followed a lovely trail. The trail was the epitome of the road less traveled. Cat people never need to take their cats for a walk. So the only person who really used the path was Gladys. She loved it that way. It was private and peaceful. The path led to a babbling brook, then a small opening between some trees. Something caught Beebee's attention and she started tugging Gladys in that direction. Gladys smiled knowingly.

"wow. such clearing. again," Beebee thought.

"Oh, want to go to the warm spot? Want to go to your special warm spot?" Gladys asked as she let Beebee lead her away.

"very warm. nice," Beebee barked.

After walking through the trees, they reached a beautiful clearing. This "warm spot" was a special place for the two ladies. It was their secret place. The sun shone on a big stone boulder shaped like a bench, made perfectly for a human to sit on. Gladys sat down and let her furry baby off her leash. She pulled out a pack of cigarettes and a lighter. Beebee looked back at her, studying her for a few seconds, then barked as if reprimanding Gladys for smoking.

"wow. such habit. bad," she thought in her doggy brain.

"First off, none of your business! Second, if I can't have kids, at least I don't have to act like an expectant mother. Now go run around, freak!" Gladys retorted, suddenly feeling a little pissed to be treated like a kid by her beloved little practice baby.

She mentally scolded herself for being so flippant, and watched in rare quiet contentment as Beebee circled around the clearing as if looking for something. She touched her tummy again, and rebelliously took a deep drag from her cancer stick.

"I gave you three fucking years," Gladys sighed scornfully, thinking about her beginnings with Roy and how they'd excitedly gone on sex marathons to get a bouncing little baby. But here she was, making do with a bouncing little dog.

Suddenly, she was startled by some rustling noises beyond the trees. A large German shepherd appeared, prancing towards her. This was a big dog that looked like it could eat other big dogs. It had no leash. Gladys was not used to being confronted by large beasts like this.

"OK, big boy. What are you doing here? Beebee, over here! Come!"

Beebee's head shot up, and she obediently followed her master's orders. The big boy pooch ran up to meet Beebee halfway and gave her a doggie kiss on her nose.

"wow. stud. plz. much more," Beebee barked.

"no choice. such training. plz help," Charlamagne huffed.

Gladys found that amusing and cute. It immediately put her at ease. She sat back down and let them continue to have fun with each other, sniffing butts and tasting privates. The private tasting left her feeling a little jealous of her little mutt. She didn't see anyone to smell her behind. "OK, big boy. If your master is handsome, and shares your greeting customs, this might turn out to be a good Sunday after all."

Standing behind Gladys, unbeknownst to her,

was a tall, dark and handsome gentleman. His name was Francis. And he looked dashing, like he had walked out of a 70s French soap opera. He had curly wisps of hair and a wide, devilish grin. Trim and half the size of Roy, Francis had a wiry wiggle to his disposition. He definitely looked European, because his clothes were a bit tighter than any American man would wear.

"Well, I did teach him everything he knows," Francis murmured almost to himself, which registered like a teasing whisper in Gladys's ear. She could feel the goose bumps at the back of her neck in response to his presence. And a tingle ran up her leg as she sensed his manliness and musky scent. As a defense mechanism, she didn't let on to her attraction, and responded roughly.

"You scared me! Sorry, it's just that I've never seen anyone in this place. I thought it was my secret find. You know, last place in America where smoking is allowed?" Gladys said, brushing her naughty thoughts away.

"No, I'm sorry. I didn't mean to scare you. And I didn't mean to ruin your buzz. Looks like Charlemagne and your doggie are getting along," Francis replied, eyeing the dogs, who had started making out rather aggressively, earning a well-pitched whistle from his pursed lips. Gladys thought it was sexy. That's how desperate she was for male attention.

"Now, Charlemagne, give that sexy bitch some room. Anyway, my name is Francis. And the reason you've never seen me here before is because I'm new to town. The first thing I wanted to do was explore the local green space, and find a place where I, Charlemagne and bad vices can run free," Francis added. He pulled out a pack of cigarettes and flipped one into his mouth perfectly, like he had practiced it a million times.

"Ha! Glad I'm not the only one," Gladys commented, making it seem as if she was staring at the cigarette and not his lips.

"We may be the final two people on earth. So, what's your name?" Francis asked as he lit his cigarette.

"Oh yeah, I'm sorry, I'm Gladys. And I have been coming here for a long time. Maybe a little too long. That is Beebee, she's my, um, child, so to speak. We live just a few minutes from here," Gladys replied, trying to sound normal and hide the girlish nerves coursing through her.

"Just a few minutes, huh? Just the two of you?" Francis asked, the words rolling sensually off his tongue. Francis looked around as if he expected another man to come along. Gladys took notice.

"Yes, no, with Roy. He who shall not know of my dirty little habit. Which I may add, is a leftover from my college days. It's the last bit of juvenile trouble I haven't been able to let go of," Gladys said, so quickly that she nearly stuttered through the words.

"How sad! With a body like that, a girl like you could get into quite a bit of trouble," Francis replied. And just like that, her naughty fantasies evaporated. She wasn't keen on men who openly made sexual innuendos to women they hardly knew in public places for all the world to see and hear.

"OK! Um, Francis, if that's your real name, hitting on women in the park, and clumsily at that, does not suit you. That's kind of rude," Gladys said.

"I'm sorry. Yes, I'm sorry, but your large breasts compelled me to say that," Francis apologized clumsily, completely throwing Gladys off. While some distant part of her brain liked his offensive and rude sexuality, the sense of propriety in her was still offended.

Gladys stood up, and fast as a bullet, walked off, screaming like a lunatic as she went. "Beebee, come, let's leave these two dogs alone! And by the way, I carry pepper spray, and if I see you around here again, your eyeballs won't be getting a chance to compel you to say shit!"

Beebee cooed in displeasure with Francis's boorishness, while eyeing down Charlemagne in sadness for this early departure. Her small dog brain struggled to process the various conflicts around her. Her instincts veered towards the slight distress in Charlemagne's behavior.

"wow. such parting. such sorrow. how rude," barked Beebee. "much parting. home. such crate. no choice. sad," barked Charlemagne in return.

Gladys walked off in a huff, stomping the ground in annoyance. As she got to the end of the clearing and near the exit of the woods, she looked back. Still standing, Francis and his pooch had not moved, and were staring back at her. She wondered if her eyes were playing tricks on her, but the two dogs, the human and the beast, seemed to be smirking at them. Francis certainly was smirking at her, while Charlemagne's look was more a glance of disappointment that his moment with Beebee was over.

"wow. white. such fluff. sorry. no choice. bad parent," Charlemagne thought.

She continued walking, passing her house once, then twice. She didn't feel like going in yet. Her favorite place was presently off limits, and her home was full of Roy. Luckily, she remembered Roy's piss poor request, and walked a little way to the beer store to let off steam. The nerve of that guy, Gladys thought angrily. She dragged the resistant Beebee, who obviously had liked the licking session that had happened so far away.

Chapter 2

The next day, the unpleasant encounter with Francis had worn off, and Gladys felt better. The weather wasn't feeling as well as she was, though. The once sunny sky had become a dreary grey, and everything outside her window seemed bleak. She didn't let it get her spirits down, though. She determinedly brushed her hair and put a little color on her cheeks before going out for her walk. She called for Beebee, who immediately responded and obediently walked her out on the leash. They walked slowly and leisurely down the street back to the local woods. It was late afternoon. The sun would set soon, but she liked the cool air of dusk.

The sunny clearing was now a rainy mess, and everywhere Gladys stepped, mud stuck to her boots. She quickly let Beebee off the leash so she could get her pooping and peeing business over with, worried to get caught in the hard rain. Beebee sniffed around her usual trees and nooks, but the rain kept getting in her eyes and perturbed her usual directness. She kept sniffing around, and with every step moved farther away from Gladys. And in a sudden moment where her doggie senses lapsed, poof, she disappeared into darkness.

"wow. very dark. plz help."

The sky got even darker, and Gladys was yelling for Beebee. She looked around, but she couldn't see her. The dark shadows and corners weren't helping at all. Beebee was gone. And there was no sound of her, either.

"Beebee! Where are you?!? Come, Beebee, come, Beebee! Come ooooonnnnn!" Gladys hollered louder as she walked deeper into the woods. Thunder struck and made her worry even more. Where the fuck did that stupid mutt go, Gladys thought worriedly. She thought she knew the woods well, but now seemed lost.

She heard something rustling in the woods and turned to follow it. Some shrubs rustled and crackled. Gladys's eyes narrowed to focus on the spot, but still she couldn't see Beebee.

"Beebee, is that you?!?"

Upon walking into an even darker and thornier section of the woods, she could hear Beebee crying faintly, suggesting she was further into the woods. Damn Beebee, why did you have to go so far, Gladys thought in annoyance, as she brushed the shrubs out of her path. It was even darker under the trees, and Gladys could barely see the ground she was walking on. Chubby raindrops fells off the tree branches onto her face. "Fuck," Gladys muttered. A few more steps ahead, she finally found what she was looking for.

"OMG! Beebee! What did you do?!? How did you get stuck in there?" Gladys asked Beebee, as she looked into the hole. Beebee was stuck in a hole three times bigger than her. Gladys hit her forehead with the palm of her hand for asking her little mutt questions as if she could actually answer.

"Crap! OK, I'm coming," Gladys said, as Beebee started crying.

"so scared. much precipitation. ur hope."

Gladys lay down on the ground, getting all of her clothes muddy and soaked. She reached down into the hole as far as she could. She had almost reached Beebee, when all of a sudden a bolt of lightning hit a tree next to her. The boom was frightfully loud and scary. It ripped apart the small tree, splitting it in two and sending one half in Gladys's direction. The small trunk fell right on Gladys's leg.

"Dammit!" Gladys cried.

The wood felt as if it weighed a ton, and it pinned her down in place. Gladys tried to lift the fallen tree off her leg, but she realized it was too heavy for her. It wasn't heavy enough to break her leg, but it was heavy enough that she couldn't move it from the position she was lying in. She couldn't get much leverage out of her arms, as they were lying in a twisted angle anyway.

"Fuck! Fuckity fucking shit balls! OW! Beebee, you little shit. I'm leaving you down there, you little asshole! OW!"

Gladys angrily hit the fallen tree with her hands in frustration. Then she remembered she was living in the new modern age and she had a cell phone in her pocket. "Let there be signal, Lord!" Gladys begged mentally. She clumsily reached for her cell phone and dialed Roy.

"Pick up! Pick up! Come on! Please. Just once, get off your ass and get the phone!" Gladys screamed into the ringing cell phone.

Meanwhile, inside their house, Roy was uncharacteristically not on his throne. Roy was at the family desk, Internet-chatting with a friend. The glow of the monitor gave his face a ghostly sheen, and he was talking animatedly into the microphone.

"Look, all I'm saying is, and I mean this 100% percent... you can take out the onion and the salami, and tomatoes, even the provolone cheese, and *STILL* call it Hoagie! Hoagie's just the general name of a sandwich around here, it don't need to be Italian at all!"

His phone lay on the desk, set to vibrate. It lit up and slid to one side from the vibrations. The screen flashed Gladys's picture. But he kept his eyes pointed straight at his webcam, intently listening to his friend's argument as if they were having the most important debate on earth.

"Can't argue with this, man," Roy said in return. He smiled and took a huge and obscene bite of a hoagie, then plopped the whole thing, paper wrapper and all, on top of his phone, conveniently blocking Gladys's picture.

Back in the woods, the sun had gone completely down, enveloping the whole place in darkness. Gladys could only see the surroundings whenever lightning struck and highlighted the nearby branches and vines. Gladys kept the phone to her ear until she heard the unfeeling recorded voice mailbox message of her husband start playing. She looked up at the imposing tree and then down at the deep black hole.

"F-U-C-K...*ER*! Beebee, the President must have called him into the situation room. UGH!" Gladys said in wry amusement as tears started filling her eyes. "I married, married, a fucking, fucking, fucking idiot!"

The rain kept pouring, soaking her deeper into the ground. Tears started spilling down the corners of her eyes as she cried quietly. "Shit, I'm going to have to call 911 or I'm going to die here. Hey, if I die here, at least we'll be together," Gladys told Beebee in despair.

Just when she had finally given up, Gladys heard a voice she had never thought she'd be happy to hear again.

"Hello! Is anyone out there?!?" It was Francis.

"You've got to be kidding me," Gladys said aloud in disbelief. Then she panicked, wondering if she'd been silent too long, and started screaming, "Um, hello! Yeah, I'm here! Help!"

Francis and Charlemagne suddenly appeared in the dark woody area.

"Oh no! Hold on!" Francis said, as soon as he saw Gladys lying on the ground. His first reaction was confusion. Why on earth would Gladys be lying on the muddy ground? Then he saw the fallen tree pinning her legs.

Francis picked up the log, and with great strength, picked up Gladys and tossed her over his shoulder. At the same time, Charlemagne craned his long neck down into the hole. Beebee jumped up. Charlemagne bit into her collar with his mouth, and pulled fluffy little Beebee up to safety.

"wow. how strong. much chivalry," Beebee thought.

"gud. so safe. gud. very glad," Charlemagne thought back.

They walked a little bit, and Francis laid Gladys down gently next to a huge stump. Francis knelt and inspected her leg.

"Are you OK?" Francis asked. It seemed bruised but not broken, Francis thought.

"Yeah, but I'd be better if I hadn't been saved by a pervert. I suppose I should say thank you," Gladys replied, sounding genuinely grateful even when she tried to sound cynical.

"Well, no. I suppose I should say I'm sorry after how I acted the other day," Francis replied, setting down her leg and looking up into her eyes.

Gladys looked away, embarrassed. "And you would suppose correctly."

"Question. Does my apology, plus saving you from violent trees, warrant a chance to start over again?" Francis replied, smiling tentatively.

"I will say this, my threat of burning out your fucking eyeballs is belayed for now," Gladys replied, as she looked Francis straight in the eye to show how serious she was. "Now, if you'll excuse me, it's fucking raining! I have to trudge home and make dinner for my superhero of a husband," Gladys said, trying to mask her anxiousness with annoyance.

She strained to get up and shook off the dirt and mud from her clothes. She wiggled her ankle a little and tested her bad leg to see if it could take her home. She found the strength to limp away, with Beebee following behind, dreaming of the ways she would skin Roy alive. Even when she thought of it, she could feel Francis's eyes on her. The wet rain made her clothes clingy on her body. It was not hard to see her top wrap around her breasts, revealing that her nipples were rock hard. The V-neck of her shirt was weighed down as well, and exposed much more than it was supposed to. A hint of her pink bra stuck out above her cleavage, and against the backdrop of darkness it stuck out like a warning flare, only calling more attention to her body.

Francis did not need much time to internalize the sexual visions before him. With every blink, he took a mental picture for his database of perverse memories and his wank-bank of sexual images.

"Put some ice on that!" Francis called out. Charlemagne barked to get the last word in.

"so saved. wow. now crate. so dark. plz," ruffed the noble Shepard.

After what seemed like an eternity, Gladys and Beebee made it home. Once inside the house, Gladys felt the fleeting contentment of a dry, warm space draining at the sight of Roy. He was staring at the flat screen as if he had never seen a TV in his entire life. She was mad, but determined not to say a single word, until she saw Roy's cell phone lying on top of a pizza box.

"What the hell!" Gladys blurted in disbelief, feeling anger wash over her in a tidal wave of disappointment.

"Huh? Hun, where have you been? I got hungry, so I ordered a pizza," Roy said, still staring at the TV. Gladys fought hard, tooth and nail, not to throw her boots at the TV. She let out a sigh of defeat and flipped open the pizza box of shame. Her heightened sensitivity absorbed every single detail: the outline of every missing slice, save for the one mocking her suddenly roaring stomach. She felt tired, helpless and angry.

"You ordered the pizza? Wow, and you saved me a whole slice! Wow, Roy, what fucking generosity to come home to! And by the way, how did you order the pizza and not see that I called you?" Gladys asked, closing her eyes to calm her nerves. Every stimulus seemed to anger her more, especially Roy's unfeeling, idiotic voice.

"I don't know. I was really hungry, I just picked it up and started dialing," Roy explained, in that same innocent monotone. Gladys felt like cutting his tongue off, along with everything else that hangs. "I saved you a piece with meat on it," Roy added, as if by way of apology.

Gladys hovered desperately beside the husband who had become nothing but a stranger to her, hoping he would glance her way to see how she felt. She'd caught a glimpse of herself as she passed the mirror on her way in, and she wondered how no one had stopped her on the street to ask if she needed to go to the hospital.

They must have seen murder in my eyes and were scared away, Gladys thought wryly. She continued to stare at Roy, who was completely under the TV's spell.

"Ugh!" Gladys exclaimed, giving up all hope. "I'm going upstairs to take a long, hot bath. I would invite you to come take one with me, but I want to fucking murder you right now!"

"What? Yeah, great. Hey, so you're not going to eat that?" Roy asked, eyeing the last slice of pizza with unmasked delight.

Gladys walked away in stony silence, giving her husband one last glance, but he was still staring only at the TV screen. Fuck it all, Gladys thought. Your loss, not mine.

The bathroom, as usual, gave her some comfort. It was the only place in the house where she felt warm and safe. She looked at herself in the mirror again as she carefully took her clothes off, studying her body, looking for injuries. Her white skin bruised easily. There were many black and blue spots from the nightmare she had lived through. I look like a fucking zombie, Gladys thought. The thought made her feel worse, and she ended up throwing her shirt at Beebee, narrowly missing her. The shirt made an ugly plopping sound as it hit the floor, like meat hitting a butcher block.

"wow. very fit. such pride. two nipples. very few," said Beebee.

"Like the view, you little peeping tom?" Gladys asked Beebee affectionately. She wanted to be pissed at her Beebee, but it wasn't her fault that Gladys had decided to get out of that horrible house even in that weather. Besides, they had gone through it together, unlike the stranger in her living room, who no doubt was now enjoying the last slice of pizza with delight.

She turned on the shower and set the water past warm, all the way to hot. Her glistening nude body started to beam with wetness all over, as the steam permeated the air. She lifted her foot inside to test the temperature of the water with her toes. It was hot now, too hot, but she didn't care. Her baby-white skin would turn rosy pink after it was over, but the feeling of the water would be worth it. It would wash away more than just dirt, but the day and all that had happened. I don't want to be angry anymore, Gladys thought, I want to stop caring.

As she entered the shower, the scalding water hit her back, her butt and her boobs. It hurt a little, but hurt so good. Steam rose in the shower, fogging up the mirror and blurring her reflection. Every drop was washing away her anger, soothing her muscles, and warming her freezing body. She caught sight of the small shaving mirror opposite the shower, fogged up like the one above the sink. She wiped it with the palm of her hand and looked into it, staring at the stranger in the mirror. Until then, she had always managed to find her fiery old self in the mirror, even if in fractions. But now, the weariness and the bags under her eyes that she could swear hadn't been there that morning made her into a completely different person. She closed her eyes longer than she intended to, trying to blink the awful look away.

When she opened them next, she caught Francis's reflection behind her, smiling wryly. Somehow, he was in the shower too, and somehow he had managed to lose his shirt and pants. Gladys confirmed what she had imagined helplessly at the back of her mind: the lone Allies cannon along the Siene was thick, broad and worthy.

"Did somebody say pizza? I got a whole pie just for you, Mon Cheri," Francis whispered in his slow, sexy voice. The smell of a fresh pizza pie permeated the air. It cut through the steam, and hints of pepperoni and crust seemed to fill her belly with fullness. Gladys could feel the warmth of Francis's breath on the side of her neck, amazingly and wonderfully warmer than the shower. Each exhalation felt like a wet kiss on her skin. His eyes stared straight into the mirror in all seriousness. Francis's hand slowly made its way from her narrow waist to her shoulders, vying with the sensual way the water caressed her skin. A little pressure on her sore muscles was all it took for her stress to wash away. This Euro apparition was real enough for her to start feeling the heat within her that she had not felt in such a long time.

"You seem tight," Francis noted, not really looking at anything but her eyes. "Let me take care of that." He kept kneading her back with his strong fingers. He must have been a fisherman, she thought. Strong hands made from hard work and manly toil.

Francis kept massaging her shoulders, pressing on all the right places. Gladys tried to hold her mouth shut, but it was sheer pleasure, such pleasure after what she had just been through, that she let it slide. Just this once, Gladys thought. She leaned forward, arching her back, thrusting her breasts forward suggestively. They pressed against the glass of the shower and made pink circles with coronas of soapy water. She peered into the mirror and saw the wicked smile on Francis's lips. Stop, or I'll kiss that wicked smile off your face, Gladys thought naughtily. Francis continued to work on her shoulders, then moved down to her back. His fingers caressed the sides of her breasts ever so lightly. Gladys couldn't help but lean closer, aching for more.

Below her waist, she started to feel something else. It was the tip of his baguette, or maybe his saucisson, now cured stiff, peaking into the loaves of her butt cheeks, looking to make a sandwich of lust.

Then, a second pair of hands appeared. This did not make sense, but she didn't care. One hand was holding a slice of pizza while the other held a cup of soda with a straw. Gladys didn't give a fuck about the food getting soaked with water. Her hunger didn't give a fuck. She ate it up while relishing the feel of Francis's hands on her.

"You are so wrong. Go away, weirdo," Gladys murmured, meaning the exact opposite.

Francis continued to massage her lower back until he cupped the cheeks of her ass. A little squeeze came next. She moaned at the goings on down below while he leaned in to nibble on her neck up above. Then he did it again. The slight pain of the pinched skin distracted her from the poke she was getting from behind. He wasn't inside her yet, but at his lovemaking pace, he would be deep in her before she could say, "ooh, la, la."

"Down, boy. We hardly know each other," Gladys murmured again. Liar.

Wait, what the fuck, Gladys thought, snapping back to reality. Two pairs of hands? Pizza in the shower? And then, splash! The sound of a flushing toilet rudely interrupted her confused mind as cold water shot out of the shower, shocking her body. She pulled the shower door open, and saw the last person she wanted to see, Roy.

"What the hell!" Gladys screamed.

Roy turned his head to face her, finally, but the stupid lost look on his face set her anger afire again. Embarrassment fell over his face as he stood there with his pants rumpled around his ankles and his wiener dangling rudely outside his boxers.

"amaze. such cock. such block. wow. hide doge," thought Beebee. "Oops, wasn't thinking," Roy blurted out, much to Gladys's anger. "Under fucking statement of the year!"

Chapter 3

Two days had passed since the shower fantasy incident. And Gladys, after an afternoon of cuddling with Beebee and watching old romance films on her computer, couldn't take any more of the cheesy lines and hot kissing scenes without thinking of Francis and that twisted trick her mind had played on her in the shower the other night. Gladys decided to take Beebee for a walk.

"amaze. how right. now. charlemagne," said Beebee.

Gladys stood at the entrance to the woods and watched the mom train pass her by. The women this morning were especially garish. They had the little tots in tow and were all carrying rolled-up yoga mats. It must be baby yoga day, she thought as they approached. They just walked around the woods, safe on the sidewalk, too scared of invisible germs and bugs to go into the woods with their little babes. They were laughing, looking adoringly at their children as if they were living the best time of their lives. Gladys wondered if she'd ever be standing before a baby's stroller in this life, instead of pulling at the end of a leash. Hatred and jealousy rose in her heart as each Stepford Wife passed her view.

"Beebee, if I ran over those bitches with my car, you think the judge would be lenient?" Gladys asked Beebee, as she hugged her close to her bosom like a little babe.

"plz. good. very likely," Beebee barked in response.

"I didn't think so," Gladys replied, even though she didn't understand doge speak. She set Beebee on the ground, walked away from the mom train, and headed for the clearing, heeding Beebee's persistent tug. It can't possibly be all sunshine and rainbows, Gladys thought cynically.

The clearing was bathed in sunshine, so different from the night Beebee had gotten stuck in the hole. She unfastened Beebee's leash to let her roam free. Gladys saw Francis and Charlemagne sitting on the stone bench the moment they walked in. He was wearing sunglasses, and the look suited him, Gladys thought, with a glint in her eyes. She brushed it off harshly, remembering her little bathroom fantasy.

"Everything OK?" Francis asked, looking at her with mixed amusement and confusion. Gladys didn't even realize he had removed his sunglasses while she was staring at him.

"You know, I don't know how the human mind works, but do you think it's even remotely possible for you to forget that you ever found this place?" Gladys asked. She understood the heat, because the sun was shining regally today, but what to make of the hot, hot blood coursing through her veins she didn't know. Better to act gruff with him.

"It's possible," Francis replied simply, crossing his legs one over the other. His strong fingers flicked around his shades while Gladys tried to suppress the vision of him holding her tight.

"Is it possible without me having to bash your head in with a rock and cause amnesia first?" Gladys asked, looking around for Beebee to get away from his disconcerting eyes.

"You are an angry woman. You need a cigarette?" Francis asked, shaking his head in confusion before slipping his fingers into his shirt pocket for his cigarette case. Those slipping fingers, what else could they slip into, Gladys wondered distractedly.

"You know what? I actually forgot my cigarettes today. So yes, if you have an extra, I'll take one," Gladys replied, and sat casually beside Francis.

"And does this nicotine charity constitute that reset of our relationship that we talked about?" Francis asked, pulling the cigarette case away on second thought. Gladys was about to blabber, flustered in thinking about what to say. Then Francis let out a low chuckle, his eyes twinkling with amusement, before holding out the cigarette case to Gladys again.

"Fine! Reset button has been pushed. But there is no relationship here, buster. There just isn't another fucking boulder in this park to sit my ass on," Gladys replied, as indignantly as she could, and lit the cigarette with the lighter Francis held out for her.

"You're funny. Look, all joking aside, the park is big enough for the both of us. And I promise, no more perverted comments," Francis said, raising his right hand in oath. Gladys looked at him for a couple of seconds, looking in his eyes for a hint of mischief. She found none.

"OK. Deal."

They smoked in silence for a couple of seconds, then Francis broke the awkward silence with a serious face that sent Gladys's heart hammering against her chest.

"So," Francis started, and puffed smoke before continuing. "What kind of underwear are you wearing?"

Gladys felt like slapping some sense into Francis's twisted brain, breaking a promise mere seconds after it was made. She wanted to think Francis was capable of sense and sensibility, unlike Roy, but he seemed to have not even an ounce of decency. But rather than slapping him, she let out a sigh of exasperation, taking a deep drag from her cancer stick.

"You know, I don't give a flying shit about your weirdness. Not today. The answer to your question is yellow," Gladys replied dismissively.

"Yellow?" Francis asked incredulously. He let a second tick by, letting Gladys burn in her own heat. "What, do you shop at the banana store?" Francis added, then burst out laughing, so proud of his wit. "Banana store!" Francis repeated for emphasis, staring Gladys straight in the eye, as if more surprised that she couldn't get the humor.

"such corn. plz," Beebee barked.

"much repeat. so same. bother," Charlemagne sighed.

"Wow, how is it that a catch like you is still single?!? With the fucking banana store sense of humor, you would think women would be lining up to hear your bullshit," Gladys replied drily, and got up from the bench, looking around for Beebee. Where's that little mutt when you need her, Gladys thought.

"You're very funny," Francis said thoughtfully, looking at Gladys with his head tilted a little to the side. "Yeah, yeah, I know," Gladys replied absentmindedly. "Can I ask you a serious question?" "No," snapped Gladys.

Francis chuckled a little, then cleared his throat, determined to ignore Gladys's wishes.

"Other than walking the dog and giving me shit, what do you like to do in this city?"

"That's not even a serious fucking question! It's like a half-flirt, even! That's a flirty question from a guy on thin ice!" Gladys exploded, her fantasies going up in bursts of insensitive flame.

"Look, I'm going into town. I don't know where to go, you know, to tell my banana jokes," Francis replied.

"Well, Mr. Banana Jokes, honestly, I don't have much of a life anymore. I work from home. My husband is never home, except when he is pretending to be a stump in the living room. I just don't feel like kicking around with the young people downtown anymore," Gladys replied, more serious that angry. She was just so tired.

"Aw, that's a shame," Francis replied. One look from Gladys's slit eyes and he raised his hands, palms facing up, as if in defense. "And I mean that seriously, not as a prelude to flirty compliments about your mammaries," Francis added innocently.

This is exactly the kind of person Roy was, and I fell for it, Gladys thought dismally. Not happening again.

"Hahaha! I'm laughing because I'm surprised you know the word mammary. Used on a human, it's the only word more vulgar than tits," Gladys replied, with a poisonous dose of sarcasm.

"Well, it's nice to see you laugh beneath that armor of yours," Francis replied thoughtfully, with a small genuine smile that tore at Gladys.

"Well, if you were a woman with these mammaries, in a world where guys like you have functioning eyeballs that compel all sorts of fucking comments, you would have some armor too," Gladys replied.

"Ha. Marvelous," Francis added. Seeing the doofus speechless was priceless to her. As if on cue, Beebee bouncily walked in between the shrubs.

"Beebee, let's go," Gladys called out. Beebee tilted her head, looking like she wanted to get back to some more of what she was doing in the bushes. Still, Beebee walked over and obediently waited for Gladys to put her leash back on.

"Later, alligator," Gladys said flatly.

"I'll be here tomorrow. If you want to meet up again at a certain time?" Francis said hurriedly before Gladys walked away.

"Um, Francis, guess I'll roll the dice on us meeting again, if that's OK with you," Gladys replied politely.

"I'll be here tomorrow. Come and see me," Francis said, with a huge smile on his face.

"Um. Yeah. Whatever," Gladys replied noncommittally.

Gladys walked away, not realizing there was a dangerous smirk on her face. Francis's amused eyes followed her back.

When Gladys reached the house, she was surprised to see Roy's cushy throne vacant. She called out, but no one answered. She heard some noises upstairs, like something heavy being dragged on the floor. She let Beebee off the leash and walked upstairs.

"Roy? Roy?"

Roy didn't reply, so Gladys opened the door and found him heaving a suitcase onto the bed. It was covered with clothes.

"What are you doing?" Gladys asked Roy, who looked at her with a blank lost face. "What. Are. You. Doing?" Gladys asked more pressingly.

"The office said I got to go up to Minneapolis. I uh, forgot to tell you," Roy replied, scratching his head absentmindedly.

"For how long?" Gladys asked, after biting down her first retort.

"Two weeks," Roy replied, looking uncertain. "Two weeks, tops," he added, when he saw the look on Gladys face.

"Husband. Husband of mine. I'm not going to give you three guesses, or two guesses. No, just one guess, to tell me what particular date of importance happens to fall within the next two weeks," Gladys flatly demanded.

Roy's eyes lit up like a boy who had gotten an A on his first test. "Our anniversary," Roy replied brightly. Then his shoulders slumped upon realizing what that actually meant. "I know," Roy added, seeing the raw anger in Gladys's face. He had no idea how often she wore that expression – he rarely looked at her at all these days.

"You know?" Gladys asked in disbelief. "Do you care?"

"Look, this is work. Since you got laid off, I got to bring home most of the money. The little side jobs you do here and there ain't going to pay for that fancy dog food. So I got to do what I got to do. They say I got to go, then I got to go. And for our special day, we will celebrate it when I get back," Roy replied seriously, which troubled Gladys more than his half-assed stupid remarks. When Roy got serious, things went from bad to worse.

"I hope we have a reason to celebrate it, Roy.

I really do," Gladys added, sounding defeated.

Roy was about to reply, when the sound of a car stopping in front of their house interrupted their conversation. Roy glanced at the yellow cab briefly, then turned his attention back to Gladys.

"Don't talk like that. Hey, look, my cab is here. I'll call you when I land," Roy said.

"Do Roy. Do call me when you land. And if you crash, don't call. Give me at least a few moments to feel relieved that you didn't make it out alive," Gladys replied flatly, though her eyes betrayed her calmness. But the cab had Roy's full attention. Something else always had his full attention.

"What? Huh, yeah, honey, I'll see you later," Roy replied distractedly, and left.

Gladys bit her quivering lips and squeezed her eyes shut to keep the tears from spilling needlessly. No one who matters will see it anyway, what's the fucking point, Gladys thought in despair. She turned back to the window in time to see Roy walk out of the gate without a single glance her way. They always look back in the movies, Gladys thought, letting her tears fall the moment the cab's door swung shut. She pulled the blinds to cover the window, turned around, and took three wobbly steps before falling face down on the bed.

"such baggage. gud. very gud," Beebee chirped.

Chapter 4

Fuck this, Gladys thought, after hours of staring blankly at the bedside table. "Fuck this bullshit!" she said out loud. She stood up, opened the closet, and stood on tiptoes to get a good look at the top compartment. She was a few inches too short to see anything. She had told Roy to lower this goddamn cabinet, that giants didn't live here. She dragged the chair over and stood on top of it. Beebee paced around the floor, instinctively knowing that such a big creature couldn't manage on top of that wobbly structure for long.

"Great," Gladys said with a mischievous smile. She pushed the other boxes to the side, looking for one special box she had thought she'd never feel like opening again. When all the other boxes had been pushed aside, at the back of the compartment, Gladys found the box she was looking for. It was labeled Single Clothes, the clothes she used to wear when she was still busy hanging out and dating. She pulled out another box labeled Fuck Me Pumps with a naughty smile on her lips. Hopping off the chair, she flipped open the box tops, sending them flying across the room. She caught a glimpse of herself in the long mirror and checked out her ass. She spanked it for good measure, as if to wake it up for what it was about to do. She set the box down for a second and gave her butt a good squeeze and jiggle with both hands.

"much jiggle. tempting. gud squeeze. no fur," remarked Beebee to herself.

"Let's get this fucking show on the road, aye, Beebee?" Gladys asked, with a huge smile on her lips. Beebee barked in agreement with a full wag of her tail.

She carefully removed her clothes and spread them on the bed. Next, she pushed all of Roy's magazines off the table and onto the floor. She kicked a bunch of them under the bed. Fuck him and his fishing magazines. Let him bend down and look for them later, she thought. Then she lined up her fuck me pumps on the bed. Beebee watched her with curiosity, sensing a drastic change in her master.

Looking thoughtfully at her old collection, Gladys couldn't help but feel like something was missing. Then it hit her. She jumped back on the chair and rummaged through the compartment for another special box, a smaller one. She found it and pinned it under her arms before carefully getting off the chair. She opened the box and stared admiringly at her collection of the greatest 90s club hits CDs. With a flip of the lid, she popped in good ol' 1997 and pumped up the volume. She started draping the dresses over her body, checking herself out in the mirror. "To fit or not to fit? That is the question," Gladys said thoughtfully, looking at Beebee for an answer. Without missing a beat, a bark came out of Beebee's mouth.

"90s. too early. not born. gud. amaze."

"But first, some wine!" Gladys shouted. Like an eager kid, she flew down the stairs and made a dead stop at the liquor cabinet. Most of it was full of Roy's brown hooch. Those bottles were full of stuff that was way too strong for Gladys's baby-soft pallet. She focused her gaze on a pink bottle in the back. It was some concoction of white Zinfandel and guava. It was called Yessir. The cover art displayed an exaggerated caricature of a sexy club girl in a teeny tiny dress. The slogan on the label read, "Shots? Yessir!"

Gladys pulled it out of the cabinet along with a wine glass. She poured as she walked up the stairs.

Turning up the music, unmindful of all the babies in the neighborhood, Gladys started trying on her dresses. They all seemed a size too small, but she could still fit them over her body. Gladys smiled at her reflection in the mirror and decided on her little black dress.

"See, Beebee? I still got it! Fuck this shit. This bitch is going out!" Gladys screamed against the stereo with a huge grin on her face.

"such squeeze. shrink. plz. wow," Beebee barked in disagreement, noting how the dress seemed too tight.

"Whatever. What do you know, anyway!" Gladys replied, still smiling, determined to keep her spirits up.

She bent down to pet Beebee, smiling like an idiot. But a loud ripping sound wiped the smile off her face and silenced the coochie-cooing of her breath. "No. No. No! No! No!" Gladys yelled, closing her eyes in disbelief. Then, she stood up, turned her back to the mirror, and looked at her worst fears brought to life. The dress was ripped from her back all the way down to her butt. The cleavage of her butt cheeks looked like an arrow pointed to her mess.

"No!" Gladys exclaimed once more, and in her frustration knocked the stereo off the table. "That was my New Year's 1998! I guess it's too small. Or I'm too big, Goddamnit!" Gladys wailed mournfully, as she collapsed on the bed. "Oh, Beebee, why?!?" Gladys murmured, as Beebee jumped on the bed with her.

"fabric. much cheapness. ur perfect!"

She ripped the dress off of her and surrendered to another wave of tears. It was more than just the dress, it was as if her hope had been ripped apart as well. The stereo was broken. Now it was just gurgling static while the disc spun inside. The white noise was calming, and Gladys let it play on. She stared up at the ceiling, looking for answers.

Beebee licked Gladys's face, first on the forehead, then on the lips. Gladys didn't usually like that, but didn't care at the moment. She tore off the remaining shreds and slid under the covers while sitting up a bit, pulling the glass to her lips and letting the Yessir drain onto her tongue. It wasn't strong, so she drank it like it was juice. And then another, and then another. The third glass went right to her head. A thumping pulsed in her forehead and her eyes were dizzy. She decided to close her eyes and let the thumping grow louder.

As she teetered on the verge of sleep, Gladys felt a warm hand caress her face. Letting her imagination run wild, she reached up and pulled at the wrist of this phantom feeler, guiding it downward towards her neck. A smile came over her. She liked it, whatever it was. Wearing only panties, she squirmed further into the bed sheet. One hand guided her intruder further down her body, while her other hand went even further. Her legs spread apart to make room for a little exploring.

A familiar voice filled the air. Francis cooed "One Banana, two banana, three banana, four!" "Hey, weirdo," Gladys whispered, "what did you get at the Banana Store today?"

Feeling an object land carefully on her tummy, she felt a familiar fruit.

"I got a sweet plantain for you, Ms.

Mammaries," Francis said. "And this one goes brrrrrrr."

Francis slid the plantain-shaped vibrator's switch to the on position and began to do the exploring for Gladys, while she sighed out loud in ecstasy. It approached the hinterlands of her fanny and hovered above its target like a drone waiting for orders. The orders came, and they said enter, breach the creamy mounds and make a banana split!

The white noise of the stereo kept humming as eventually Gladys slid into dreamland, drunk and satisfied.

Chapter 5

The next morning, Gladys woke up groaning. Her eyes burned the moment she opened them. The toxins in the Yessir still had a hold of her brain. She ignored the hangover with determination, and hopped downstairs to wake herself up with a cup of hot coffee. She pulled a hoodie over her head, then rummaged through the mess for yesterday's pants and tops. After putting Beebee back on her leash, Gladys grabbed her fresh coffee in her hand and dragged Beebee out of the house. Not going to mope in that hellhole for another fucking minute, Gladys thought determinedly. The door swung open and she bolted out into the world.

Unfortunately, her brain was still hung over from crying her eyes and wits out the night before. Fuzzy memories popped in and out of her head. In her frustration and tiredness, she rounded the corner distractedly, running smack dab into the mom parade. Beebee's leash got stuck on one of the baby stroller's wheel. Gladys didn't notice it, and continued to walk on. Fortunately, Beebee pulled against her.

"how rude. plz. such wife. trophy. unprepared. wow."

"What?!?" Gladys demanded, getting the attention of the mom train. Only then did she notice the leash stuck on the wheels. "Dammit, Beebee,"

Gladys muttered.

"Excuse me, aren't you going to get that?" asked the mom train member.

Gladys looked up and met the eyes of the baby stroller's owner, a rather attractive red-haired mom. Gladys couldn't help but compare herself to the red-haired mom, who spoke distractedly into her phone, not even bothering to take care of the stroller tangle herself. Gladys winked at Beebee and let the uppity mom wait while she drank her coffee.

"Um. Excuse me," the red-haired mom said, holding a hand over her cell, "Your dog is tangled up in my baby's stroller. Can you get him off? He's getting upset. We're late."

"Well, your baby is going to have to learn some patience," Gladys replied flatly, before taking another sip of her coffee.

The red-haired mom pocketed her phone with an exasperated sigh that got on Gladys's raw nerves. "Excuse me," the red-haired mom said, as she gently pushed Gladys aside to untangle the leash herself. "Here, I got it." Gladys noticed the red-haired mom's outfit. It was a nice flashy hoodie and sweats set that hugged this

momma's figure perfectly. She looked comfortable and sexy, and was in no danger of suffering the same humiliation Gladys had privately suffered the night before. It was a bit much for a morning stroll, but the times had changed on this street, and fancy was the default position for these housewives.

"You're lucky that I'm not the kind of person who gets angry," the red-haired mom said as she untangled the leash, taking her time. She stood up and brushed the dirt off the palms of her hands. "And if you don't mind me saying so, you really need to settle down, because your negative energy can be felt by children as young as three months. And there are a lot of young children in this neighborhood who could be affected in the wrong way by an angry dog walker," the red-haired mom added.

"Dog walker?" Gladys asked incredulously. "Excuse me. I live here, bitch! I've lived here longer than you have!"

"Well, I wish our realtor had given us a better assessment of the kind of people in this neighborhood. My Sally needs to have an atmosphere of positive thinking, good intentions and good vibes. Believe that!" the red-haired mom added, struggling to speak as calmly as possible in front of the other moms who stood watching a few feet away. "Please excuse me, I'm late in meeting my friend at Starbucks."

"plz. much waste. too leisure. wow. what

rush," thought Beebee.

The red-haired mom stormed away, clicking and clacking her heels against the pavement. Every sound drove the nail deeper into Gladys's nerves, and when she got to the woods, she was even more flustered than before she'd left the house. Poor Beebee couldn't help but let Gladys drag her on, hoping she would find a good place to vent and let her off the leash.

"do vent. so near. charlemagne. wow."

Passing the perfect houses, down the long street, they finally made it back to the clearing. Then Gladys let Beebee go free. She looked around for a couple of seconds, telling herself that it was a relief to find the place empty. She took a dog toy out of her pocket. "OK, Beebee, catch!" She threw it a few feet away, but Beebee stayed seated, tired from all the pushing and pulling. "OK, you want a liver treat? Go get it!"

Beebee stared blankly at Gladys, then turned around and looked to the woods. Gladys felt guilty for dragging her around. "Aw, you miss your furry friend?" Gladys asked, as she slumped on the ground with Beebee, who barked in agreement. "Yeah, me too. Don't know why."

After 20 minutes of sitting around in the sunshine, Gladys and Beebee were back at home. Gladys sat on Roy's sofa throne, trying to balance a bowl of healthy breakfast mush on her stomach like Roy did. But the bowl kept tilting sideways. Gladys laid it on the table and grabbed the phone to dial her sister, Pam.

"Sis. Pick up, it's me. Just wondering what you guys were doing. Maybe we can hang. Work on the garden or something. Like, drink a lot. OK? Call me, love you!" Gladys said into the phone, as she stared sadly at the TV she hadn't realized was turned off.

She turned on the TV while trying to balance the bowl on her stomach again. She heard a narrator's voice mention John F. Kennedy's name. Her head shot up, and she stared at the TV, wondering if she was hearing things.

"Kennedy was a known philanderer, often sneaking women into the White House..."

Gladys clicked the remote to the next channel. It was a cooking show competition. The sudden appearance of sliced livers jolted her to click again. Now it was a tennis match. Then a mega preacher, then a space cartoon. She grew bored with the TV quickly, and threw the remote down. There was nothing good on.

She slowly got up, looked around the house, and settled on some cleaning therapy. She cleaned the house in spurts while taking breaks to fart around the Internet and check her phone for her sister's response.

Pam did not call back, or even text. Boredom set in. Confused about what to do, she looked to Beebee for answers.

"very time. do try. early. too surrender."

The little dog was not ambivalent about what she wanted. She was tapping at the door, hoping to give it another go in the park.

"charlemagne. such knight. much armor. fur. wow."

"Aw, gee whiz, Beebee! I know you wanna go back out there, but we were just there!" Gladys said. Beebee was unfazed, and started yapping now that she had her master looking in the direction of the door. Small in size, Beebee looked so serious that it was as if she was staring down her master.

A staring contest commenced between the species. The big doe eyes of Gladys versus the tiny black dots of Beebee's. Gladys let out a nostril-heavy nose huff, and Beebee responded with a heavy chirp. Like in the showdown in a Sergio Leone movie, one of these wills had to give to the other.

The silence swelled until Gladys blinked and started laughing. "I'm going to cook you into glue someday, squirt. You win," Gladys said. Beebee barked again and started pawing harder.

"wow. win. very satisfying. amaze."

Gladys picked Beebee up and went for the doorknob. She hesitated for a moment. Gladys took a huge gulp of air and turned the knob, almost jumping out of the house with determination.

Together, Gladys and Beebee made their way to the local woods again for the second time that day. They walked a little and jogged little. Gladys couldn't shake off the mix of anxiety and excitement she was feeling. Beebee could hardly be restrained by the leash.

"much chance. charlemagne. do arrive. gud," Beebee thought.

Within a few minutes, Gladys found herself in the woods, unprepared for what was about to happen.

Sure enough, Francis was there, sitting on the stone bench, while Charlemagne sat by his feet, patiently waiting. His head shot up when he heard Beebee bark.

"beebee. much hope. do remain. help," he thought.

"Ah, my girls!" Francis said, with a twinkling in his eyes. Gladys slowly approached, not really sure how to proceed.

"Good grief, just when I wanted some peace

and quiet." Gladys said, as she feigned annoyance. She knew she was breathing too hard to pass off her lie, though.

"Right, right. Hey, we're just playing a game, want to play with us?" Francis asked.

"OK. Whatever," Gladys replied, with a sigh of relief.

"Great," Francis said, with a goofy smile on his face. The smile sent the butterflies fluttering in Gladys's stomach – a feeling she hadn't felt in a long time. She had no idea what game he was talking about.

"What kind of game are you playing?" Gladys asked nonchalantly, as she watched Beebee and Charlemagne sniff each other's privates deeply.

"Oh, it is a game I learned when I was a kid. It's called bet the girls and win some kisses," Francis replied.

"Bet the girls and win some kisses?" Gladys asked skeptically. "Were you a seldom winner or often loser?"

"You have no faith in me," Francis whispered, tickling Gladys's ear.

"None whatsoever," Gladys muttered, trying to look indifferent, not that it worked. Francis watched her with unmasked amusement, which strangely left Gladys feeling like he was stripping her naked in his mind.

"Here is the game. If I can get Charlemagne to kiss Beebee, then you have to give me a kiss," Francis explained simply.

"No chance. No chance! No chance in hell, ever, ever!" Gladys replied.

"Why? What's the big deal?" Francis teased, leaning closer so their lips were a mere inch apart.

Gladys took a hesitant step backward, stalling while she looked for her wits. "First, um, ew! Second, I'm a married woman," Gladys explained, her voice trailing at the end when she realized how lame her excuse sounded.

"And where is Mr. Gladys?" Francis asked, one brow raised in question.

"He is in Minneapolis. So that's still in America, and that's still being married, and you're still a perv," Gladys explained without stopping for a breath.

"Well, I don't see what the big deal is," Francis replied, taking a step back himself. "When was the last time anyone begged you for a kiss?" Francis asked, as he looked at her sideways.

"Begging? I don't see any begging," Gladys said, looking around as if to prove her point. "My dog kisses yours, I get to kiss you," Francis said, ignoring her comment. "You're nuts!"

"Are you afraid?" Francis asked, his hand cupping his chin while a finger toyed with his lower lip.

"Of what?" Gladys asked innocently.

"Of liking it," Francis replied, his full luscious lips spreading into a wide, confident grin.

"I will not like it on a house, I will not like it on a train, I will not like it on the mouth, and I will not like it fucking EVER!" Gladys bit back, her face turning red in embarrassment, knowing she was overreacting.

"What if you were single, would I still have a chance?" Francis asked, his face turning serious.

"If I went to a women's college, and was drugged out of my mind, and there was a war that killed off all the other men? Maybe," Gladys replied with amusement. Looking around for Beebee, she thought she caught a glimpse of Francis's eyes darkening a little.

"Well, it seems like the lesser species is a bit less choosy," Francis replied dismissively, and only then did Gladys see that Beebee wasn't simply kissing Charlemagne. They were going at it like hyperactive teenagers copying porn films. She had thought they were just hanging out like buddies, but this was no buddy- buddy situation.

Charlemagne's larger frame was mounted on top of Beebee. His paws were massive compared to hers. His hind paws dug into the dirt, while his front paws were crossed in front of Beebee. She was holding on for dear life as she spread her paws out wide, trying to stabilize her body. The visuals were primal, and the sounds matched. Charlemagne's pleasure-crossed eyes gave him a goofy grin for a dog. Slobber was flying in all directions. It was almost comical.

"Hey! Get off her!" Gladys yelled nervously at Charlemagne. She could feel her heartbeat going faster.

"Let them!" Francis replied, not even bothering to hide that he found the scene exciting.

"Your dog is raping my dog," Gladys said pointedly, staring dubiously at Beebee, wondering how dogs could fuck each other so aggressively and quietly.

"No, it's their animal instincts. The call of the wild compels them," Francis explained like a scholarly monk, making Gladys wonder if perhaps he actually was an actor.

The canine lovemaking was starting to reach its apex. Charlemagne's humping sped up. He was now bucking forwards into Beebee's cotton ball body in a blur. Beebee started yelping, and her suitor started howling. Then, as the runaway train of carnality reached top speed, it went off the cliff. And then they instantly stopped together, with a slight whimper sneaking through their sharp teeth.

Charlemagne pulled out and hung back as if to rest. He reclined on his back like a good dog sitting for a portrait. Gladys's eyes widened, despite all attempts to keep them from doing so, when she saw Charlemagne's secret lure.

"What is that?" Gladys asked in a mix of confusion, curiosity and disgust. "Ah, here it comes!" Francis murmured excitedly, as if he didn't hear Gladys at all. Gladys watched as a little willy came out of Charlemagne's already engorged shaft. "EW!"

"That," Francis began like a professional tour guide, "is his second penis. It lives in his first penis. Now wait, it gets better. Watch." Francis grabbed Gladys's shoulders when she started to turn around to make sure she saw. Gladys watched helplessly as another willy came out from the hole of the second. Charlemagne proudly got up and mounted Beebee again for a second round to ease his insatiable lust.

"That's his third penis," Francis explained unnecessarily. "Can you feel the heat?" he whispered as Gladys watched, so dumbfounded that she seemed to have lost her wits permanently.

"No, just barfed in my mouth," Gladys replied sincerely, the grimace on her face making an honest woman out of her.

"Tic Tac?" Francis offered like a caring and sensitive friend.

"Four, please," Gladys replied. She wasn't exactly in the mood to see reality.

As Gladys watched them angrily, Charlemagne continued his handiwork. With a shudder, Gladys recoiled. She had never actually watched copulating dogs from beginning to end. Francis's dog stepped back and pranced around as if he had just been transformed into a stud. He smiled dog ear to dog ear, and Beebee smiled back. She was proud of her champion Sheppard. Since dogs didn't smoke cigarettes, the post-sex pillow talk session was short. Charlemagne got up and pranced off. He obediently returned to Francis, like he had done it a million times before.

"gud boy. much dinner. earned light. gud," he said to himself.

With that exit, Francis started walking away, giving Gladys's shoulders a passing sensual squeeze.

Gladys closed her eyes in surprise, feeling exactly the way she'd felt in her fantasy when Francis gave her a fuck massage. "See you tomorrow. You owe me a kiss," Francis whispered in her ear for a sensual goodbye.

Gladys was still reeling from what she had seen, felt and heard. It took three full seconds before she could retort, "In your dreams!" Angry about having lost her poker face several times, she snatched up Beebee and walked out of there in the opposite direction. She had barely walked ten steps when she felt like she had a bull's-eye on her back. She spun around just in time to catch Francis with a devilish look on his face. Just when Gladys thought she'd caught him off guard, Francis waved at her like a sailor on a ship, gave her a flying kiss and walked away. "Great," Gladys complemented herself cynically, frustrated and pissed that she actually did feel the heat.

Chapter 6

Hours later, back in her bed, Gladys cuddled Beebee, who had been sleeping since the second they got home. Who could blame little Beebee? She had just had the ride of her short little life. Gladys glanced down at Beebee when she heard her little mutt whimpering in her sleep. Her little muzzle fluttered as air sputtered out.

In her dog mind, the world was black and white, but the pleasures were shades of gray. In a field where the grass was made of jerky, and the trees dropped marrow chunks like acorns, Beebee sat alone on the finest silk pillow. A runway made of pork hide was before her, and at the long end of it was her champion. He strode tall, fur forward, nose high. Facing her, he started to run faster, swinging his penile trinity to and fro. When he arrived at his final destination, he came to a full stop. And nose to nose they met, and understood the best was yet to come.

"much humping. very steady. plz," begged Beebee.

"too right. wow. such playing. came," responded Charlemagne.

From there the world of canine carnality turned, season to season, dusk to dusk, penis to second penis to third penis.

"Good dream? Or nightmare? What's it gonna be for us, girl?" Gladys asked quietly, staring into space. "At least you got some. Got some alien-looking penis," Gladys thought aloud, with a small smile creeping onto her face as she drifted off to sleep herself. And not long after, she was in the heart of dreamland.

"Either you get that fucking dog off the bed or you get on the fucking floor, baby. What's it gonna be?"

The booming reverb-filled voice bounced off of the bedroom walls like a cathedral's echo. Gladys sat up in surprise, waking and pushing Beebee off the bed in the process. The room was different. The flowered wallpaper from the delicate deb collection was replaced with a paisley print of concentric dog boners. The art in her room was different. No longer were there scenes of serenity and baying foxes, but artfully rendered paintings of Francis's smirking face. A couple of paintings were of his hairy chest and hairy butt, deep crack and all.

She rubbed her eyes in disbelief for a couple of seconds, telling herself Francis had not followed her home. But his voice was real.

"Good girl," Francis's voice said, followed by footsteps in the hall. Moments later, the fresh Frenchman moseyed to the door space. He was wearing a white robe that was too short for his frame. It was cut so high that the pink helmet of his swinging noodle peeked out from the bottom. He pulled a tie off the robe as he slowly got onto the bed. He lay down on his side, facing Gladys, who was still in shock. His robe was now open. The truth was growing and getting bigger.

"What are you doing here?" Gladys managed to ask.

"You owe me, from the game," Francis innocently replied, his innocence betrayed by bodily gestures. With his head propped on his right hand, Francis let his left hand roam free, first feeling Gladys's smooth, creamy legs under her nightgown. This is not happening, Gladys thought, more excited than panicked.

"Yes it is, dog lover," Francis responded, as if reading her mind.

In a sea of reverb and chorus, the room started to change. The reds got redder, the boner art got bonier, and the hairy butt paintings got fuller and hairier. Francis leaned closer to catch Gladys's eyes and held them, while his hand traveled up in a slow, torturous caress.

"It's OK, honey, you can close your eyes," Francis whispered, brushing his lips softly against Gladys's ear. Gladys, hypnotized by the hundreds of sensory neurons telling her to go get fucked, closed her eyes obediently. Behind her closed eyelids, Gladys saw Francis's shadow moving about. This was not anatomically possible, but any grounding in reality was thrown out the window as her desire willed it so. Then, she felt some sort of fabric over her eyes. Francis was blindfolding her. Soon after, her view was cast into darkness. The visual world was no more. She could only hear with lustful ears.

Gladys felt Francis's weight shift as he left the bed. Gladys could hear him going through the drawers quietly, like a thief in the night. For a split second, Gladys felt panic and tightness rise to her throat. Just in time, Francis got back on the bed, trapping Gladys between his legs.

"What are you doing?" Gladys asked, her voice hoarse and ragged.

"Improvising," Francis replied, his voice penetrating her eardrums. On cue, Gladys felt a cold steel object on her thighs, followed by the sound of scissors cutting her nightgown. The cold steel teased her nerves as she pictured Francis's tongue in its place.

Gladys drew a sharp breath when the scissors slipped under her panties, slow and cold on her warm wetness.

"Like that, hmm?" Francis asked as he slowly ran the closed scissors between her legs. Within a second, Gladys's panties were gone. Francis quietly continued to cut Gladys's nightgown until her body was completely exposed. "So, what do you want first?" Francis asked, not really waiting for an answer, as he ran his hands over her thighs, all the way up to give Gladys's breasts a tight squeeze, before going back down to spread her legs again.

Gladys held her breath in anticipation as Francis shifted on the bed again. "Hmm, shame to let all that honey go to waste," Francis murmured to himself, but loud enough for Gladys to hear. Oh my god, Gladys thought, her imagination running wild. She could feel Francis moving closer, slowly, until she felt his tongue between her legs, licking her hard clit hungrily.

"Oooooh," Gladys blurted in pleasure and surprise, her hands finding their way to Francis's hair. Her fingers tightened and pulled at his hair, at the same time pushing his head deeper into Cupid's gorge.

After a few minutes of lapping her maple syrup, he turned his face upward with force.

"More of that later, dear, in the meantime, behave," Francis replied, moving around the bed again. Gladys could hear the scissors cutting something again, then she felt Francis's hands on her wrists, tying her tattered nightgown around one end. There was only one logical assumption as to where the other end would go, Gladys thought, as Francis raised her hands in the general direction of

the headboard pillars. After tying her hands on
the other side, Francis gave her a deep, penetrating
kiss, his tongue still tasting of her. Suddenly,
everything went quiet. Francis's tongue left her
mouth, making its way down her neck before
suckling her nipple like a baby left unfed for three
days. Gladys grabbed her makeshift chain
helplessly, wanting to pull Francis closer against
her, closer until his man-thing sank fully inside her.
She could feel her dripping wetness again, and then,
as if he heard her thoughts, Francis left her tits
behind and raced his way down again. This time,
he lapped it up harder, like a dog eating gravy.

Gladys couldn't hear anything other than her
ragged breathing and her heart pumping blood
through her veins. She wondered how Francis
could fuck her so quietly, but there really wasn't
much room for wondering, as her brain seemed to
have lost functionality, every single brain cell
dedicated to feeling Francis's tongue on her clit.

Then, she heard her cell phone ringing. The
room changed again. The walls fell away. An
indoor earthquake shook her fantasy loose.

"Wait," Gladys said, as she tried to get away
from Francis's grip on her legs. But Francis didn't
respond, and kept at it. The ringing grew louder
and louder, until Gladys couldn't bear it any more.
She screamed for Francis to stop, and when she
finally opened her eyes, she was tangled in her bed
sheets, alone in her bed with nothing but the echo

of another subconscious suggestion. She had even managed to get her hair tangled in the headboards.

"I am so fucked, aren't I?" Gladys asked Beebee, who was still sleeping at the foot of the bed like the most peaceful mutt on earth. Gladys groaned upon hearing her phone ring again, and pulled at the knots frantically. She was able to break free and kick off the covers to pick up her cellphone on the 10th ring. It was her sister Pam, returning her call.

"Pam, I am so fucked."

Later that day, they were sitting on Pam's porch, hoping it would give them enough privacy to talk about Gladys's predicament. The noise from a kid's birthday party was enough to shield their conversation from young ears. Regardless, Pam kept a close watch on the door for her husband, Gary. Gladys, on the other hand, fixed her eyes on her sister's kids, little colorful bouncing blobs in the kiddie pool. Gladys took one long look at Pam, seeing the resemblance between them. She couldn't help but reminisce about the times they had borrowed each other's clothes and talked all night about boys. They were always walking down the street in their fuck me someday but not yet pumps, hand in hand, making sinners of boys and men alike.

"Sooooo. What's the big ass news you

wanted to tell me? Are you getting a divorce?"
Pam asked Gladys.

"No," Gladys replied, rolling her eyes at her
sister, who always managed to assume the worst
about her relationship with Roy. Pam had always
thought Gladys shouldn't have married Roy. But
then again, she had never thought anyone was good
enough for either of them. Which is why Gladys
had thought it was a huge miracle when Pam
married Gary.

Gary was an alright guy. He sold cars, ate
the same breakfast every day, and managed to keep
track of his matching socks. He was an everyman,
but he was kind and he loved Pam, and that was all
that mattered.

"Good bye. Come back when you get
divorced," Pam replied, still the spitfire inside
despite her age.

"Pam!" Gladys begged, more in amusement
than worry. She knew her sister meant well, despite
the bitch she always wore for a second skin
whenever she got a chance to get away from her
kids. "No, I am not getting a divorce. But I have
something that will get your eyebrows raising,"
Gladys explained, pausing to check her sister's
reaction. Pam was looking murderous, expecting
more juice. "I met an interesting man," Gladys
finished hesitantly, making it sound more like a
question than a statement.

"Well, you're definitely not talking about Roy," Pam replied with a wicked smile on her face. She looked around once to check if anyone was listening. "And? This story better get dirty and good fast!"

Gladys took a deep breath before rambling on, her nerves making her sentences nearly incoherent. "I met a guy that has a dog at the place where Beebee and I go that no one goes to. And he's super handsome and taller than Roy and more handsome than Roy. But at first I thought he was a total creep! Like he made crack about my boobs the first time we met, but then later, he kind of saved my life in a rainstorm where a tree fell on me, and he used his superhuman strength to get it off. So he gets a pass for the creepy boob comments and somewhat redeemed himself by being kind of charming and I think he likes the idea of banging me right there in the park." The second she finished, Gladys took a big gulp of air, clasping her hands on her lap like a teenage schoolgirl waiting for her friends to approve of her crush.

"Well, first, whoa!" Pam replied with a sly grin on her face, her eyes wide with excitement. "Now, banging you in the park, I understand. Getting his face between your mammaries I understand, bending you over a wild oak tree—"

"Pam!" Gladys interrupted before Pam could plant more images of Francis doing stuff to her. She already couldn't get any peaceful sleep because he kept popping up in her dreams with his handsome grin and lean, muscular, naked body. "So, he asked me to kiss him, like straight up asked me to," Gladys finished. Pam rolled her eyes and gave herself a face palm.

"And you in your endless row of chickenshit decisions decided to say no. And you passed on making out with a strange man in the park. Deep down inside you don't want to be a ho. Deep down inside you wanna be bent over the wild oak tree by a strange man over there. And deep down inside you kind of wish Roy would know about it for a millisecond and understand how he neglects you, but then immediately forget about it so you don't have to live with the guilt and you can still be the good girl who never wronged a wrong in her whole life," Pam rambled.

"Still haven't," Gladys replied, an attempt at humor to console her sister. "Still boring, sis," Pam replied, shooting her a deadly glare. "Hey kids! Stop that! Take that out of your mouth! Spit it out!" Pam suddenly blurted out, off topic. Gladys turned to see what her sister was so vehemently rejecting and saw one of her kids removing her foot from her mouth. "Is that a whole foot?" Gladys asked in disbelief.

"My child is very talented," Pam replied proudly. "Look, I think you need to sprinkle a little spice in your stew. Like pepper. Make the stew good with some naughty action. Just carry mace.

Or that little gun Roy has, you know, just in case the strange man turns out to be a creep. Then you're going to have a hell of a story to tell. From jail," Pam added seriously.

"Pam!" Gladys objected, forgetting everything but the words gun and jail. "So, do it?" Gladys asked hesitantly.

"Do it," Pam replied decidedly and with finality.

"I can do it. I can do it," Gladys chanted, as if to convince herself. "Now that I have your permission and Roy is not even around, one kiss wouldn't hurt me. A kiss never hurt anyone," Gladys added, her voice trailing off at the end with doubt and anxiety. Then, as soon as she was on her way home, the anxiety turned into full- blown excitement.

Chapter 7

The next day, just as the sun was beginning to set, Gladys found herself sitting on the stone bench beside Francis, wearing a tight mini skirt and a spaghetti strap top to go with her red fuck me shoes. The outfit was hot, but the fuck me shoes kept digging into the ground. Francis wore a costume of a douchy dude with wingtip shoes.

They had been sitting there for five minutes, watching a repeat performance from Beebee and Charlemagne. The huff and the puff of fur and slobber flying acted as a backdrop for the witty banter between the consenting adults. The conversation was above reproach at first. Dogs, weather and the latest news dominated. Then the ice was broken by Francis's gruffness.

"Hey, I brought some pot. Wanna smoke?" Francis asked, holding out an ominous looking drug.

"Some what?" Gladys asked, trying to hide her surprise in case she came off as an innocent little school- girl.

"L'Herb de life my dear. Don't tell me that you have never had a hit of pot before?" Francis asked, not even bothering to hide his condescending surprise. So you think I'm miss goody two shoes, huh? We shall see, Gladys thought naughtily.

"I have once, back when I was a bit of a wild child. On my 20th birthday. Janine Hanson made some pot brownies and brought them to my party and I ate a whole one! It kind of made me feel dizzy. I never really saw the attraction to it, especially since most of the pot smokers of my youth were smelly-assed slacker types who never amounted to anything," Gladys explained, shaking her naughty thoughts out of her head.

"Come on, chickenshit, have some. Quit stalling," Francis replied, holding the joint out for her.

"I'll have some if I want to. I can totally handle it," Gladys replied, more to herself than to Francis. She pulled the fresh joint to her mouth and inhaled. She tried to hold it in like normal cigarette smoke, then started coughing profusely, bringing back painful memories of her first days as a rebellious smoker.

"Ahh. Ugh, that's really fucking horrible," Gladys commented, making an effort not to screw up her face.

"Whoa, hmm, let me try again," she said.

An hour later the two of them were on the grass, laughing like they'd just heard the most hilarious joke ever. Francis propped himself up on his elbow to roll a fresh joint while Gladys was enjoying the last bit of the first one. She smiled like she had never smiled in her entire life.

"And so I said to him, that's the smallest penis I have ever seen. If it were a type of pasta, it would be called petini! So then he gets this smug look on his face and takes my cell phone off the dresser and wipes his butt crack with it! Then he makes noises like a donkey, grabs his clothes and leaves. Funny, but I saw him like a year later on the train with a total babe. She must eat petini," Gladys rambled on. Her thoughts were a loose jumble floating in her head. She could see Francis finish rolling another joint out of the corner of her eyes. She could see him watching her with that devilish look on his face. Gladys was sure that if she just gazed in the general direction where his cock was, it would be boulder-hard, because she could feel herself dripping wet and getting wetter all the time.

"It's a good thing you don't like petini," Francis murmured, leaning closer to nibble on her earlobe.

"If I don't like petini, what do I like?" Gladys asked absentmindedly, her brain cells focused on his tongue, reminding her of her dream the other night.

"I have no idea, but I have every intention of finding out," Francis replied as he tilted her face to his and drowned her lips in a deep, slow kiss. His hand traveled down to pull her hips against his as their mouths meshed together in a hot, wet, sloppy kiss. True enough, Gladys could feel him against her, hard as a piece of iron. For a moment she felt embarrassed, knowing he could sense her wetness from her heat. But with another tug at her hips and a slight grind against his sausage, she forgot about the embarrassment. Just when Gladys thought he was about to get her naked, Francis pulled back, cradling her face in the palms of his big, wonderful hands. He was staring deep into her eyes.

"I see you," Francis said out of nowhere.

"What the fuck are you talking about?" Gladys asked harshly. She'd had enough of his teasers. She could barely hold on and survive with her pride intact when all she could think of was pushing the fucking bastard on the ground and riding him senseless. And now he was trotting out some philosophical bullshit.

"I see the true you. The you that needs to come out more," Francis replied, as his eyes toured down her body. On his way back up, he leaned in too soon, grazing the tops of Gladys's breasts with his chin, and he lingered, brushing her tits softly with his thumbs. Their eyes met and locked.

"My name is Francis Moore. You will say my name. Francis Moore," Francis said, like a psychologist putting a patient under hypnosis.

Gladys couldn't help but smile when she realized what he was doing; he was torturing her, he was hypnotizing her, he had her drugged with his sheer will.

"Your name is fucking ridiculous," Gladys replied, unintentionally putting too much emphasis on the word 'fucking'. Another long silence went by with their eyes still locked together. Then Gladys, surrendering to his dirty fuck me mind tricks, leaned in first and their lips locked together as their tongues danced. Francis propped himself up on both arms on top of Gladys without breaking their kiss. He found the small of her back and pulled her so they were sitting facing each other while Francis fumbled for the hem of his shirt. They only let go when Francis pulled the shirt off over his head and flung it away. Gladys confirmed what she'd first seen in her bathroom visions and then in the bedroom. She could find not a single ounce of patience left to wait; she wanted that body on her naked skin.

"Damn, nice abs," Gladys thought aloud. Francis's lips spread in a confident smirk. "We will make sex now, yah?" "I should say no," Gladys replied.

"But you won't." "I should go home." "But you don't want to."

Not necessarily, I'm quite torn between taking you on my bed and staying here, Gladys thought, making up her mind. "No. I don't want to go back," Gladys replied, "so just the shirt, Francis? Come on, Francis, more!"

Francis stood up, unbuckled his belt, unbuttoned his pants and lowered the chastity zipper, all while Gladys sat watching his little strip performance in the best seat in the house. He lowered his pants with his boxers and his pole was revealed, like a soldier standing in attention out of respect for Gladys's war zone, pointing at her face seductively. After taking her top and bra off, Gladys slipped her skirt off, and down her legs she flung it with the rest of Francis's clothes. For a couple of seconds, they stared at each other's nakedness, their eyes burning with lust.

"Not bad, Francis Moore," Gladys said appreciatively, slowly lying back on the ground as she did so.

"Not so bad yourself," Francis replied as he followed her down. He parted her legs with his knee and held them wide open. With a pull, he could feel himself against her, and she was ready.

Beebee and Charlemagne watched as Francis licked her clit before suckling it, a million times better than what Gladys remembered from her dream. She grabbed a handful of his hair for support and started riding his mouth. He moved higher, wetting her stomach with her own juice, before he moved upward and pressed his dick into her in one slow, full thrust. Their lips locked in a kiss again, as Francis grabbed her hips to keep her in place while he fucked her senseless, the way he'd seen her begging to be since she'd walked over. Gladys grabbed his shoulders, burying her face in his neck. She could hear herself, loud in the silence of the park, but she didn't care very much, she wanted more. She bit him on the neck. A little mark was left, but she didn't care. Like a shark, she marked him for a later feast.

The progression of sexuality reached a crescendo. Francis's hair was all messed up now in a doofus hairdo, and so was Gladys's. And when the climax arrived, it arrived for both of them. Lightening shot through their bodies, causing flaying arms, pointing toes and biting lips. And with spinning eyeballs, Francis howled and Gladys yelled, "Yes! Yes, you bastard!"

Spent and tired, Gladys and Francis fell like weak birthday balloons back down to earth. They lay on their backs staring at the moon that had come out before the stars.

"Now that, my dear, was impressive," Francis said. "Glad no one walked over and found us. Like a school bus full of kids," Gladys replied. "Honestly, I wouldn't have cared."

"Me neither."

Silence followed, and the woods owned the

stage as the wind rustled the leaves, which made their own percussive love songs like the two unperturbed humans had.

"So what now?" Gladys asked.

"Next time, we'll take it to the next level," Francis replied, reminding Gladys of her fantasy with the scissors and makeshift chains.

"What level are you talking about?" Gladys asked matter-of-factly. "You have no idea," Francis replied, with a naughty grin on his face. "Check. Got it."

Gladys sat up to get her clothes, but her eyes recoiled, and in a burst of bitter bile, she barfed all over the grass. Splorch!

Chapter 8

The next day, Gladys stood in the middle of the living room eyeing her handiwork. Every surface seemed to gleam, which made Gladys wonder if perhaps maybe it was her eyes that sparkled and thus made everything she looked at sparkle in turn. She had spent the whole morning cleaning, restlessly moving about, fixing everything that seemed even remotely out of order, just to help her pass the time. She couldn't wait for the afternoon, thinking about taking Beebee for a walk and Francis's promised next level of ecstasy. Even Beebee could sense the atmosphere and obediently stayed out of Gladys's way, knowing it would only delay her next visit to horny Charlemagne.

At half past twelve, Gladys had just finished a long bath. She didn't see Francis in the bathroom again, but she could feel him where he'd touched her the night before. She stepped out of the bath and stood naked in front of the mirror, admiring her assets and mentally noting how to take care of her less appealing features. She wrapped a towel around her, rummaged through the dresser drawers for something to wear, and decided to go simple. She grabbed a tight-fitting shirt and shorts that fell just eight inches from her low waist. She checked her reflection in the mirror, making sure her breasts weren't a jumbled mess by adjusting them in her bra. She turned from side to side to make sure she looked positively devastating, determined to get the upper hand later. Torn between comfortable rubber shoes and her fuck me pumps, Gladys thought about their height difference and how difficult it would be to fuck her against a tree if she was to wear the flat rubber shoes. She slipped her feet into the pumps, grabbed Beebee's leash, and attached it to her collar before going down the stairs in a blur. She checked her reflection in the mirror downstairs one last time, and gave herself a congratulatory nod before reaching for the doorknob, when to her surprise, the door swung open. And Roy walked in.

"Hi," Roy greeted her with a waning smile on his lips. "Hi, honey," Gladys replied, thankful for her subconscious mind taking control. "Where are you going?" Roy asked, giving her a once over and settling down on her fuck me pumps. "Why are you here?" Gladys asked, pretending to care and still be mad about being left hanging.

"I live here," Roy replied, still staring at the fuck me pumps. "I live here with a woman who never wears those heels for me. Where are you going?" Roy added, with his brow raised in suspicion.

"I'm going to take Beebee out for a walk," Gladys replied automatically, adding a little bitterness in her voice to remind him that he neglected that duty.

"In that outfit?" Roy asked again, staring at her tight-fitting blouse. It threatened to rip open and spill her breasts out.

"Yes. I feel like dressing up, that's not a crime! People look good in the park, why shouldn't I look good too? What, are you afraid that men will ogle me?" Gladys bit back, suddenly acting nervous and concerned.

"Ha! No," Roy replied, short of laughing at her like she just said the most ridiculous thing on earth.

"Why not?" Gladys wondered, imagining how shocked her husband would be if he knew what she was doing yesterday, and what she was determined to do when she left the house.

"No one is gonna ogle you around here. I was just wondering if you were going to meet some guy or something," Roy replied absentmindedly, as he walked past Gladys into the living room. "Well, you wanna come? Make sure there are no guys in the picture," Gladys asked, trying as best she could to hide the panic in her voice. "No, I'm gonna change into sweats and watch some TV," Roy replied.

"Why are you home again?" Gladys asked, suddenly irked that her husband would prefer watching TV to watching her in that outfit.

"Long story, it's work shit. You don't need to know," Roy replied.

"What if I want to know?" Gladys asked.

"Nah. Have fun on your walk," Roy replied dismissively. With a tinge of anger and hurt, Gladys banged the door behind her, determined to feel nice and wonderful with whoever could make her feel that way.

Why is he back here anyway, Gladys thought, as she stood ponderingly outside their house. Maybe somebody had seen her and called him, Gladys thought, with her throat locking in dread. Then she dismissed the thoughts, reminding herself that she shouldn't care what her husband felt anymore, considering that he never gave a rat's ass about her. She walked straight to the park.

When Gladys got to the clearing, her heart sank, because Francis and Charlemagne weren't there. She'd figured it was a standing date, and that he would be there from now on at the same time. It took her a few seconds to notice a small gift box sitting on the side of the stone bench. She approached it hesitantly and looked around before opening the package. It was red, with a green bow, and a lid that came off easily.

Meticulously placed inside the box, sitting on the bottom, was a small mirror. And on that mirror were three straight lines of cocaine. There was a note. It read, "snort." She stared at the contents of the box, remembering what had happened yesterday, her heart instantly beating faster, making heat course all over her body.

"Beebee, tell me what to do," Gladys asked Beebee, who looked as dejected as her upon finding the place empty. There was no doggy equivalent gift for her. So Beebee just sat silently, moping on the ground.

"sniff. such colombian. how human. very bored," Beebee thought.

"Well, fuck-all Beebee, you're no help. So, the choice is snort or go back home to watch Roy be himself. Well, fuck-all Beebee, no turning back now," Gladys said.

Gladys started snorting. First one line, then another. Then a few sneezes and a shiver. And finally the third and fattest line of the fine Columbian. As the sunshine started to bake her skin, she felt the urge to lie down and let it start up her body and mind. Pissed at Roy and pissed at Francis, Gladys looked up at the sky in annoyance.

"Beebee, click your heels and whisk us to a cool club with lots of interesting people. And interesting men and conversation. And a younger-looking ass on my backside and bouncier mammaries," Gladys rambled, feeling the rise of a cocaine buzz speed up the clockwork in her head.

When she closed her eyes, she drowned in snapshots of Francis and how he'd sexed her up really well last time. Gladys felt herself getting wet just thinking about it, and in a few more minutes she couldn't bear it anymore.

With her eyes screwed shut, Gladys reached down into her underwear, slipping a finger between her legs to feel her clit. There it was, standing at attention and begging for caresses. Her legs spread wider in response as she pressed harder, her back arching, her breasts looking for attention. Letting go of the mirror, Gladys lifted her shirt and started squeezing her own breasts, wishing Francis was there to lick her again. Holy shit, this cocaine was amazing.

In the thick of the woods, holding a telescope, Francis was hiding, watching Gladys's every move with a sly smile on his face. The perverted voyeur held the telescope steadily, watching her obedient ass break the law. He watched her patiently. Beads of sweat formed on his face from the rise in blood flow. The excitement of peeping was making his heart race. And soon enough, his free hand went for a walk downtown and did some exploring around the southland of his balls and roundabout up to his throbbing cock. He watched as Gladys spread her legs wide and slipped her hand under her clothes, touching herself in Francis's absence.

His solo pants party reached its grand finale.

Disregarding the future gooey mess and the finality of coming in his pants, he stroked to and fro until a geyser of little white future Francises shot out of his canon. This would leave a stain. He didn't care.

Meanwhile, Gladys writhed in pleasure as her clit hardened. She pressed harder. Her nipples swelled, and aroused in the same way as when Francis suckled them. And soon enough, she came hard too, and her limbs dropped limply on the green, green grass of home. Bored and pissed for having to do that to herself, Gladys got up and left huffing, not knowing that Francis was watching and tingling himself as well.

"so weird. very human. wow," Beebee thought as she sat alone.

Back at home, the light of the television could be seen through the window. If people were to pass by, they'd know for certain that Roy had returned simply by the sound of a football game permeating the street. Gladys stood outside, lost and confused, imagining her husband sitting on the couch, staring at the TV. The curtains were drawn and she knew there was not even a 1% chance that Roy would see her standing there like an idiot. That thought relaxed her. She could swear she smelled her crotch all over her body, and she was so coked out she could hardly utter a coherent sentence.

Gladys sat on a small bench in front of the

gate, hoping to sober up before dinnertime. But in a flurry of confusion, anger and other pent up emotions, the moment she put her head in her hands, tears started spilling from her eyes. One of the mom patrol bitches rolled her stroller across the street and saw Gladys. She avoided her gaze, but their eyes still met for a brief second, until Gladys broke the spell by burying her face back in her hands. Her heart raced faster and a small droplet of gooey drool formed at the base of her mouth. She didn't notice it at first, then it fell off to make an incriminating spit stain on her leg. The neighborhood had fallen silent. The sun was wilting. Down at her feet, Beebee put her head down into her paws, in solidarity with her master's pain, confusion and drugged-up brainwash.

Chapter 9

ONE WEEK LATER

Gladys looked around the house and felt like she was in her sister's house. Pam had come over with her kids, and within an hour, it looked like a family home. The place was crawling with her kids' toys. The table was filled with food, open bottles of Prosecco and orange juice. Preoccupied by alien territory, the kids were too absorbed in their games to hear a word of what was being said. Pam and Gladys felt at ease talking about Gladys's life making a turn for a movie-of-the-week ending. Gladys was doing small tasks around the house while Pam watched the children, trying her best to make sure there would be no permanent damage.

"Nothing? You haven't seen him in a week?" Pam asked for the third time after hearing about their steamy sex episode at the park.

"No. It's so weird," Gladys replied, as she absentmindedly washed a mug for the second time. "I don't have his phone number. I don't even know if Francis is his real name. This really sucks! And since Roy got back, things have been really weird with him, too. And as pissed as he makes me, at least he semi-talked to me before. Never thought I'd miss his behavior. You know what else? The mail comes every day a little after Roy leaves for work. Nothing came for me all week. I'm so mad I didn't get a piece of junk with my name in it. It's like time stopped and I'm stuck in a looped dream. It's a loop because the strollers go by like clockwork, and then he comes home and after a big deep breath I'm awake again. And there's nothing to look forward to. I'm scared this is it."

Pam looked at her sister, and for once felt she was seriously on the brink of something really bad. She'd always thought Gladys complained too much, but she'd had such a roller coaster ride the last week that she just might fall off the tracks and crash. "Honey, you know being a mom is not all it's cracked up to be," Pam replied.

"This isn't about me having kids anymore, Pam. It's about me not having anything. And yes, I'm bitching in this nice house, and shit, some women have a guy who beats them or have no home at all, but shit, I feel like bitching because I'm really not happy anymore! I can bitch if I want to," Gladys bit back, angry with herself and yet unable to stop.

"Yeah, honey. Go ahead. I won't stop you," Pam replied softly, trying hard not to over-console her sister in case Gladys got the idea that she was pitiful. If anything, that would definitely push Gladys over the edge. Her pride always got the better of her.

"Thanks," Gladys replied, as she grabbed some tissue off the table and dried her hands with it.

"Honestly, I'm not surprised about this situation with Roy. Frankly speaking, Gary changed too, little by little from the moment we got married through every year since then. Sometimes I wonder if he's still the same person, and sometimes he shows that he is. Most times though, and that's why it hurts really bad, he's just like this strange boarder who comes and goes as he pleases, paying rent as is his duty, and cares nothing for anyone else in the house," Pam said, almost in a whisper, surprised that after being married for five years, she had finally told someone that all was not well in paradise.

Gladys was just about to reply when they heard a loud crashing sound, followed by the kids screaming at the top of their lungs. Pam and Gladys ran to the living room where they found Roy, dressed in his golf clothes, lying on the floor. It was obvious that he'd fallen down the stairs.

"Holy shit! Roy, wake up! Wake up!" Gladys yelled repeatedly, as she lifted Roy's head onto her lap while Pam called 911. Gladys watched as her husband lay so still, like he would never move again.

The ambulance came ten minutes later, whisking Roy away in a gurney after securing his back and neck. Gladys rode in the ambulance with them, while Pam ushered the kids into the car to drive them home, promising to follow to the hospital as soon as Gary got home.

Five hours later, Pam sat with Gladys in the waiting room. She looked anxiously about, holding Gladys's hand tightly. Gladys looked absentmindedly outside the window at the park far in the distance, unmindful of the other people in the room who were also waiting. A few seconds later, a middle-aged rotund gentleman walked into the room. Because he looked more like a schlub than a doctor, no one noticed him. He walked purposefully towards Gladys, his face unreadable.

"Excuse me, Mrs.?"

"Nelson," Gladys replied immediately. "I'm Gladys Nelson," Gladys added, choking on her husband's last name.

"Yes. Ma'am, your husband is in stable condition. He's very lucky. He had a minor heart attack, but he's going to be OK. Unfortunately, he hit his head pretty hard when he fell down the stairs. He hurt his eye as well, and we are afraid that there may be some nerve damage, which could affect his eyesight and his balance. That, along with the heart attack, well, suffice it to say he's going to need your help to get around for a little while," Dr. Franks patiently explained.

"What's a little while?" Gladys asked, trying to get everything the doctor just said right in her head. "A couple of weeks, at least," Dr. Franks replied.

"Waaaa!" Gladys exclaimed incredulously.

"Ma'am, he will need help," Dr. Franks said gravely, but with a face that said he understood what her reaction meant.

"It's complicated," Pam interjected, as she gave Gladys's hand a reassuring squeeze.

"Ma'am, I've been a doctor a long time. I've seen my share of husbands with heart attacks come in here, and I've seen my share of distraught wives. And, 'waaaa', let's just say it's not the first time I've heard that. And that look on your face, I've seen that before, and I've seen it pass. Ma'am, when it's time, you'll take your husband home. And trust me, you'll know what to do," Dr. Franks replied, sounding more like a monk than a doctor.

"Smother him in his sleep," Pam whispered, when she thought he wasn't listening. Gladys rewarded her sensibility with a sharp elbow in her side.

"I heard that. And yeah, I've seen that, too," Dr. Franks replied, leaving the sisters to exchange baffled looks.

Chapter 10

ONE WEEK LATER

Gladys pulled up in front of their house and took a deep breath before stepping out of the car and rushing to Roy's side to help him out. He had lost his balance and had difficulty walking when he first regained consciousness, but after a few sessions of physical therapy, he got some of his balance back. They stopped for a couple of seconds outside the gate so Gladys could open it before proceeding to the house. Tired from the journey to the parking lot and car, the drive home, and the walk across what Roy had always thought to be a rather tiny lawn, they took the stairs one step at a time.

"OK, just another baby step. Come on. There you go, big boy. OK. Just another step. Last one. A few more to bed. There you go," Gladys murmured encouragingly as she held on to his arm.

"Wow, it's like we live in the top floor of space or something, this takes forever," Roy said as soon as they got to the top. He leaned on the wall for a minute to catch his breath before walking inside the bedroom he'd sorely missed while staying in the hospital.

"Clever, Roy. Top floor of space. Maybe your injuries have opened a funny pocket in your brain," Gladys replied as she fixed the bed. She came out to assist Roy in as soon as she was finished.

"No, just screwed me up really bad," Roy muttered, in a mix of annoyance and amusement. "Thank you. I'm good now, I wanna rest," Roy said as he slowly collapsed on the bed. Gladys pulled the covers over his legs.

"So, you wanna eat something?" Gladys asked.

"In a little bit," Roy replied, closing his eyes.

"You know I can make you something?" Gladys asked, her brow arched in question. She had never been a great cook, but she at least knew how to fry an egg.

"Yeah, it's that or you carry me back up the stairs after I make a grilled cheese," Roy replied, his eyes still closed. Gladys watched a small smile creep onto his lips and wondered if he was really happy.

"I can make you a grilled cheese," Gladys bit back, almost petulantly.

"Hold the spit," Roy replied, his lips parting into a wide grin. A second of silence ticked by. "Honey, that was a joke," Roy added, in case Gladys was offended.

"Hm. Ha, funny," Gladys replied, feigning annoyance.

"What, you spit in my food once?" Roy said.

"More than once. In my defense, you had it coming," Gladys replied, her lips spreading into a wide grin as well.

"Did I now?"

"Do you remember that one time on our anniversary, we were at Roberto's? We had just ordered the wine, and as the waitress was bending forward to pour the wine, you leaned in to check out her boobs. Then you asked her for her name and kept complimenting her on what a great server she was. And how if you had a restaurant you would hire her in a minute. Well, when you went to pee out your boobie wine, I did stuff to your pasta!" Gladys rambled on as she sat at the foot of the bed, smiling wanly as she remembered the old times.

"Did that make you feel better?" Roy asked, more out of curiosity than spite.

"Yes," Gladys replied, laughing a little. "But I still hurt. Why do you do shit like that?"

"Hon, I'm sorry. I don't know what to say," Roy apologized and to Gladys's surprise, he actually sounded sincere.

"Hey, it's OK," Gladys replied. She checked

to make sure he was settled comfortably on the bed. "One grilled cheese coming up. Get some rest."

Gladys did as she promised, and strode upstairs with two grilled cheese sandwiches and two glasses of iced tea. She watched silently as Roy ate his sandwich like it was the best thing he'd ever tasted, making cracks about hospital food as he did so. Gladys set the tray on the floor and watched as Roy looked around the room as if he had never actually looked at it before. After his eyes finished their tour, his gaze settled on Gladys, and a small, tentative smile spread on his lips. Gladys knew what he was trying to say, and accepted it with equal hesitance, not really knowing what the coming days would bring.

Gladys spent a lot of time reading the sports section to Roy, and when they had gone through it all, Roy told Gladys where his secret stash of books was hidden in the room. He asked her if she felt up to reading to him some more.

"Let's get you cleaned up first," Gladys replied, as she pulled the covers out of the way and helped Roy out of the bed. She gave Roy ten minutes by himself to preserve his dignity before knocking on the bathroom door to give him his medicine. He was sitting on the side of the bathtub, tired after standing in the shower.

"I know you hate taking pills. But stop your bitching. OK? It's not so bad," Gladys said as soon as she saw the grimace on Roy's face.

"But I think they are little bugs," Roy replied, eyeing the small round pills with distaste.

"Roy, your state of decrepitude is the only thing stopping me from smacking you right now," Gladys said, her voice calm and soothing to a deadly point.

"My decrepitude, or... love?" Roy asked jokingly.

"Take your pill Roy. This medicine is making you act normal in spurts," Gladys replied cynically.

Back on the bed, ninety minutes later, Gladys closed one of Roy's books. The thick book shut heavily with a thud.

"OK, that was one hell of a bedtime story," Gladys noted, as she stared at the back blurb of the book. "It was all about hell," Roy added. "Yes. Autobiography of Evil," Gladys agreed. "Part 2," Roy finished with a grin on his face.

"The shit you read, Roy," Gladys replied, staring at the book and back at her husband. "All these years I had no idea. I mean, I saw the covers and the titles, and secretly hoped you had girlie mags under the these dusk jackets."

"Cool, huh?"

"Glad I can't get pregnant, or we'd be stuck with Rosemary's baby," Gladys replied, as she returned the book to the box.

"You been taking my funny pills?" Roy asked suspiciously, with a smile on his face. He has been smiling a lot lately, Gladys thought. She smiled a little.

"Shut up and go to bed," Gladys replied.

Roy rested his head on the pillow and Gladys got up to turn out the light. As he closed his eyes, she leaned in, and planted a feather-light kiss on his forehead. Goodnight, Gladys whispered in her mind.

Gladys crept quietly downstairs and turned on the TV, her brain still wide-awake after hours of reading. She turned the volume low, remembering how she often stayed up late listening to Roy's endless marathon of sports channels at night. She started flipping through the channels and ended up on a news show. The anchor was a grandfatherly gentleman named Reese Roberts.

"And in health news, a newly released study in the Journal of Behavioral Medicine found that people who are treated with kindness during a recovery period often recover from their injuries 20% faster. Here to report is Olivia Roberts..."

While the less-dignified part of Gladys's

brain wondered how the anchor and the
reporter could have the same last name, the rest of
her higher thinking wondered if this was by any
chance another cruel trick of fate. She sulked into
the couch with a pensive look across her face as
she watched the attractive Olivia Roberts report.

"Thank you, Reese, this study finds that
people heal faster when they are treated well by
their loved ones. Kind words and gestures seem to
affect the brain more than expected. This is even
true for patients that are unconscious..."

Beebee looked up at her innocently. Then,
as if she heard something, Beebee started wagging
her tail and ran for the door. Gladys watched her
paw at it, feeling a sense of déjà vu creep up on her.

"What's up, funny face?" Gladys asked.
Beebee jumped on the door, forcing Gladys off the
couch so she could shut up her cute, insensitive
little mutt in case she woke up Roy. Beebee was
almost somersaulting in excitement.

Gladys opened the door slowly and saw
Charlemagne standing in the middle of the quiet
street.

"wow. very trained. champion. gud,"
Beebee thought.

A streetlight was right above him, and it
looked like he was on a stage with a spotlight on

him. Beebee rushed out to meet him, and they played in circles, happy to see each other. Charlemagne's neck swayed back and forth as he enjoyed his moment of freedom away from his master.

"no crate. such freedom. gud. beebee. gud," he purred.

Gladys walked up to the two lovebirds and saw a small note pinned to Charlemagne's collar. She opened up the note and started reading. "Sorry, been busy. Our place. Tomorrow? High noon? –F," Gladys read. "Fucking great," she muttered with a frustrated frown on her face.

She stood listlessly in the middle of the street trying to process. The bedroom light from a house across the street came on, calling Gladys back to the present world. She turned around, and with all her might tried not to run back into the house, but rather tiptoed on the sidewalk. Beebee stayed put, and watched Charlemagne hesitantly prance away.

"much sorrow. crate. plz. sorry."

Every ten steps he would turn his head to catch a glimpse of his friend and lover. Then he would hang his head in shame, and eventually he disappeared into the darkness. Beebee whimpered and followed Gladys back to the house.

"Uh oh," Gladys murmured, as she caught a silhouette of a person by the window in the last moment before she closed the door. By then it was too late.

She knew things were about to get even more complicated. She quickly turned off all the lights in the house, ran upstairs and jumped into bed. Roy stirred at the commotion but did not break his slumber. Gladys pulled the covers over her face, closed her eyes and counted sheep. Tomorrow was coming.

Chapter 11

When Roy woke up, he saw something he had never seen before in his life: a breakfast tray by the side of his bed. He looked at Gladys, who was smiling at him and sitting next to him.

"OK husband, here's your breakfast! I think I'm gonna take Beebee on a long, long walk today. Get a run in the park too. You keep chilling, and I'll see you in the afternoon. Maybe you can think about what you want for dinner? Yeah. Mmmm, anything you want" Gladys rambled on, managing not to trip over the words as she spoke.

"Gladys, you shouldn't have," Roy replied, but he admittedly felt touched.

"Ooooh, don't go saying all that, Roy. Eat up," Gladys said as sternly as her nervous heart could muster. Roy obediently picked up the fork and knife and started munching, while Gladys looked around the room, surprised to see that there were actually pictures of them scattered on the walls showing happier times. They had been there for years, but the smiles had not been repeated in real life.

"What happened, Roy?" Gladys asked, still looking at the pictures. Roy followed her gaze and smiled fondly at the pictures. He remembered them, but they were fuzzy, like a fading memory.

"Time. Time passed. I got older and meaner and... I don't know," Roy replied sadly, regret visible in his eyes. "So did you."

"Yeah. Sucks," Gladys replied, feeling a little guilty. She had always managed to blame Roy for everything that happened to her, and it made her feel bad to hear Roy share blame she never had any intention taking responsibility for in the first place. "I see these women walk around and I think that they have some super life."

"They don't. They really don't. Believe me," Roy interrupted, with something resembling a grimace and a smirk on his face.

"How do you know?" Gladys asked curiously. "I play golf with their husbands. When we get together, the truth comes out," Roy replied.

"Wanna share some truth, buddy?" Gladys pressed. "I'm not supposed to."

"I don't need names. Just some juice. Something to make me feel better," Gladys begged. "Well, one of the husbands is secretly gay," Roy replied finally. "How do you know?" Gladys asked. "Because he's fucking another husband!"

"What?!?"

Roy gave Gladys the look, the one that says 'why do you ask me questions and not believe the answers?' Gladys gave him a smile. "Yeah. They do it in the sports club," Roy added.

"They, uh, have gay sex in the sports club?" Gladys asked.

"Honey, why do you think guys join a private club with a hotel? A hotel, when they have homes a mile away? To fool around behind their wives' backs. They meet their chickies or dudes for some cheating sex," Roy explained, as if he was talking to an innocent child. Gladys's reaction was nowhere near innocent.

"Look at my face. See this look on my face? Say something to make this look go away," Gladys said coldly.

"I don't do that," Roy replied plainly.

"Really?"

"I got you. You are better than any woman. Better than all of them, and I don't need to fool around with some brat. I may be a lot of things, but that's not one of them," Roy replied seriously.

"Roy. How nice," Gladys replied, trying to sound cynical, but in truth, she was deeply touched. So deeply touched that what she was about to do in the woods nagged at her conscience.

"I know, I don't let you know how great you are as much as I should," Roy added. "Not nearly as much," Gladys corrected. "Not nearly as much,"

Roy admitted apologetically. "You love me?" Gladys hesitantly asked.

"I always loved you. As much as a dipshit like me can," Roy replied.

"You're not a dipshit. I think of you more as a doofus," Gladys replied jokingly.

"Thanks," Roy replied sarcastically, but he was smiling, really smiling. He felt like he'd just pulled a thorn out of his side.

"Now eat," Gladys ordered, giving her husband one good look, wondering if there was still something there worth saving. With a heavy sigh, she stood and left with Beebee in tow.

Gladys took Beebee for a walk, and what usually took no more than ten minutes took her double that time to get to the local woods. There were lots of stops and starts. She stood at the entrance hesitantly and glanced at her watch. She was nearly two hours early, enough time to think and make up her mind.

"Come on girl. Let's go to our place again," Gladys told Beebee.

When they reached the clearing, the peace and quiet Gladys was hoping to find flew out the window as she saw Francis, the person she thought would save her from her predicament, with another woman.

Chapter 12

"Uh. Hi!" Gladys said, her mind reeling. She was torn between trusting Francis and feeling betrayed, and so she took the only path open to her, confirmation.

"Oh, Gladys!" Francis replied, smiling at Gladys like they were nothing but close friends. Like nothing happened, Gladys amended.

The mystery woman, Maria, stood out, Gladys thought, with the intention of showing off her looks. Maria was like a darker version of Gladys. Great body, boobs and butt, all in bouncy proportions. She was a real stunner in any man's league. She wore a gray wool skirt and black cardigan. It was a pretty conservative outfit, and definitely out of place for someone casually taking a dog for a walk in the woods.

"very tart. wow. much makeup. average," thought Beebee.

Gladys gave her a once over, and felt annoyed at how she had wasted the effort to do her hair and make- up. This looked like it would be a huge let down.

"Hello. I'm Gladys." Gladys confidently held out her hand, giving herself a pat-on-the-back for winning that small feat.

"I'm Maria."

"You guys having fun?" Gladys asked, still fishing, still giving Francis the benefit of the doubt.

"We were just taking our dogs for a walk," Francis interrupted.

"I haven't seen you around here. And then your fucking note! Where have you been?" Gladys asked, her voice rising ever so slightly.

"You guys know each other?" Maria asked, futilely hiding her surprise and annoyance. "We fucked right where you're standing," Gladys replied, with a sweet smile on her lips. "What's she talking about?!?" Maria asked Francis, this time without pretense of indifference.

"Honey, that's when a man puts his hoo-hoo-diddy in the cha-cha," Gladys answered for Francis, who was still struggling for words. "Um. Anyway, where have you been?" Gladys asked, turning her attention to Francis.

"Grow up Gladys. You are two hours early, by the way. Look, we're adults here. I went away to do something. I'm making new friends. Why are you acting like a jealous child?" Francis asked in annoyance, but to Gladys he looked more like a lost dog caught by animal control.

"Because—"

"We didn't have anything!" Francis interrupted in frustration. "I thought a big girl like you could handle it. But I guess I was wrong."

"Huh," Gladys whispered for loss of words.

Not one to ever be at a loss for words, Gladys found herself tongue tied as her eyes started burning with tears. Insulted and embarrassed, she turned around without another word and stormed off. Beebee stayed for a few seconds and barked at Francis, as if to reprimand him for his actions. Then she followed her master.

"wow. much asshole. very doomed," thought Beebee.

Back in front of her house and more lost than she'd ever been, Gladys looked to Beebee, hesitating, still making up her mind, torn between her options. But this time, her options were different; either she would tell Roy or not.

"I'm sorry, Roy," Gladys said, practicing the words she was determined to say. "See, it's not so hard. I'm sorry, Roy."

Beebee barked, consoling her master.

"Fuck! Beebee, what an asshole! OK, here it goes."

Gladys walked up to the house, her feet trembling as she forced them to keep going forward.

She was confronted by the sight of Roy sprawled on the couch, his legs covered by a blanket. She'd thought she would have the short trip to the bedroom as a sort of reprieve, but there he was, staring at her in confusion. Then, without thought or hesitation, the words started spilling out of Gladys's mouth. What followed was a diarrhea of filth spilling into the bedroom. The tawdry tales of her misbehaviors shocked Roy. But he could only sit stunned in silence. Her expletive-filled diatribe was approaching in its denouement. And then, plunk, she ended it loudly with a shout.

"I... I... I'm sorry!"

"Whoa," Roy said, his eyes drifting from his distraught wife to the television screen. For once, he could see nothing there. For once, even though he wasn't looking at Gladys, he could only see her face.

"I didn't want to tell. I mean, I did. Holy fucking shit, Roy, and then I just saw him, and then he was a total asshole!" Gladys rambled on, tears spilling from her eyes.

"I'd have a heart attack, except I already did. Whoa. Honey, what the hell!" "It was only one time! I'm sorry. You must hate me." "Did I drive you to this?" asked Roy.

Gladys sat crying on the sofa, her hands covering her mouth to stop it from spilling more hurtful words. She beat herself up, cursing herself mentally for subjecting her husband to such cheating after he had professed his faithfulness just moments earlier. As if it wasn't enough that he'd just gotten out of the hospital, he now had this to chew on. His silence killed her, and she thought with despair that if ever there was anything worth saving between them, it was now long gone.

"Uh! My body hurts," Roy said finally. He looked at Gladys, felt pity for her and a tinge of anger. But when he thought about it, the one he really hated was himself. "I hurt too much to hate. I couldn't hate you anyway, even if I tried. I can't ever be mad at you."

Gladys looked at Roy, her eyes wide with disbelief. Then more guilt upon realizing that Roy was back, the man she'd married was sitting in front of her, hurting from her folly.

"What did he give you, again?" Roy asked, strangely suspiciously, Gladys thought. "He said it was weed. He said it was special. The other time was cocaine," Gladys replied.
"Motherfucker!" "What?"

"I don't think it was just weed! It was probably some ground-up sex drug or some shit. That's why your memory is fuzzy," Roy explained.

"It was blue. Bluish."

"What, the weed was blue? Or the cocaine was blue?"

"Both, I guess."

"There is no such thing as blue weed! Have you ever seen blue marijuana in the movies?" Roy asked her exasperatedly.

"No? But you know how there are, like, green peppers and red and yellow peppers? I thought it was like that."

"I'm going to kill him, thanks for telling me where he is," Roy muttered as he tried to get off the couch.

"Sit down Roy, you are in no shape!"

"I'm fit as a fiddle!"

Roy tried to get up, only to collapse shamefully back on the couch. Gladys looked at him, begging him to stay. He took a deep breath and pulled his strength together, pulling his ass off the couch.

"Sorry, Hon, I'm doing this," Roy answered, his face set with determination as he stood, his legs visibly wobbling. Regardless, he leaped forward, brushing Gladys's arms away when she tried to pull him back. He put on his pants and shoes and lumbered closer to the door. He was a slow-moving giant, and nothing could stop him.

Roy walked through the neighborhood, his mind so busy keeping his feet moving forward that he could think of nothing else but the bastard who'd taken advantage of his wife. If I could get that son of a bitch and kill him, then maybe I could forgive myself, Roy thought.

Chapter 13

Francis and Maria were alone in the clearing. Talking and laughing as they sat with their arms intertwined. She gazed into his eyes, captivated by the bologna coming out of his mouth.

"There are three willies, you see. They work together," Francis explained.

"I shouldn't be, but I'm so intrigued," Maria replied.

Out of nowhere, Francis screamed out in pain as a rock flew through the air and hit his back. It made a thud against his spine and hurt like a motherfucker.

"What the fuck! Oooow!"

Roy stood tall at the entrance to the clearing, his face grim, leaving Francis without any doubt that the strange man meant business.

"Who the fuck are you?!?" "I'm Roy, Gladys's husband," Roy replied, while wheezing and puffing for air and strength.

The shit was about to get real.

"Hey, hey, hey, man, I didn't know! I, I didn't know she was married!" Francis explained, looking every bit the dethroned Prince Charming.

"Yeah you did. I know because she told me so. And that's good enough for me. You're the prick that drugged her up. She told me everything. I'm gonna make your face black and blue. I'm gonna make your legs and your arms and your ass blue!"

"Hey, can't we talk about this?"

"No, we can't talk about this. We can fight about this. And you'll lose!"

Maria ran backwards away from the whole scene. She made a big semi-circle around Roy, trying to get behind him. He paid her no mind as she ran far away from him and Francis. He was intent on dealing with Francis, and Francis alone. By now Roy was right up on Francis. They were breath to breath.

"wow. very just. such knave. gud," thought Charlemagne. He just stayed put and let his master get his just deserts.

Roy and Francis stared at each other angrily. Francis wondered if Roy would make good on his promises. Roy wondered if he could make good on his promises without keeling over in exhaustion. Eyeball to eyeball, they squinted at each other.

Roy knew that there was no turning back. Before him stood his shame. His neglect. His fault. Possessing only a fraction of his strength and faculties, he would have to get creative. His only ace was his large size. He possessed one hundred percent of that.

Fast as a bolt, he threw his hands around Francis's neck and pushed as hard as he could. The force threw Francis backwards and flat on his ass, all while the grip of Roy's mitts tightened. The full weight of Roy's mass fell on top. Ribcages collided, but it was Francis's baguette basket that cracked under the pressure. The sound of the crunch shocked Francis as much as it hurt him. He pushed back at Roy, slammed his fists against his back. But all the struggling was for naught, as a red-faced Roy was burning all his gas in one last spurt.

Francis screamed for help.

"Charlemagne!"

But the simple mind of his companion had chosen from the paths of fight and flight, and chosen the latter. He didn't understand the conflict before him, but he had no reason to protect Francis. A dog's prerogative is to be always faithful to his master. But years of using Charlemagne as a tool, rather than loving him like a pet, had destroyed any loyalty to the pancaked crepe screeching for his life before him. Charlemagne stepped back. And one step at a time, he walked away from slavery and towards freedom. Crates, never again.

"AAAAAAAHHHHHHHH! Help! Stop!

Please stop, you asshole! Help me, you stupid mutt!" Francis screamed.

Roy shimmied higher up, pushed back and slammed Francis's head against the ground. Small pebbles in the dirt cracked against Francis's skull. Francis, overcome with pain, writhed on the ground helplessly. He moaned and breathed quickly, looking straight up, his eyes frozen in terror.

With his hands still squeezing ever tighter, Roy made his last advance.

"Guess she never told you what I do. I'm the motherfucker jerks pay when they need something done. And most of the time I only talk to people. Funny. Regs are like that. It doesn't take much. Just lean in and be assertive. Most people will fold and give you what you want, sign what you want. They are so scared to crack a nail or get their suit dirty. Slimy little shits like you take a lot less. But today, even with this broken heart in me, I'm gonna go the extra mile! I'm gonna try for that corner office and take some overtime on you!"

Charlemagne was obviously a lover, not a fighter, and certainly not the protector that he seemed. From a distance, at the edge of the dense woods, he watched Francis lose for the first time. Then he ran away in fear and disgust as Roy raised his head, tightened his arms and slammed downward on the knave's neck. Crunch. That show of force took everything he had. Roy had nothing

left. He collapsed and lost consciousness.
Everything went black.

Chapter 14

Gladys sat between two policemen in the waiting room of the same hospital they had brought Roy to when he'd had a heart attack. She was holding a bag of snacks. She was looking at the park again, like déjà vu, only this time she was thinking of the man she'd married, instead of the asshole he became. Just then, Dr. Franks, came in with the bad news.

"You know he was not in the right shape to be choking anything. It was just too much for him. Ma'am, I'm sorry, but your husband didn't make it. His heart gave out. He's gone." Dr. Franks explained.

"He's not going to prison, huh?" Gladys asked, with a wry smile on her face. "He's not going, no," Dr. Franks replied. "Are you OK?"

"And the other guy? The pervert?" Gladys asked, ignoring his question.

"Well, Roy had one gulp of strength left in him, and when he brought that head down, well, let's just say Francis's brain is damaged to the point that he will be leaving all women alone from now on," Dr. Franks explained. Gladys looked at him, lost and confused. "Punch drunk, to the nth degree," Dr. Franks added.

"Punch drunk? Wow," Gladys murmured.

The policemen stood up calmly and walked away, sighing in relief that they could go home. Then Gladys was alone in a room full of strangers hoping for life and death. She lowered her head into her snack bag. A small whimper escaped her lips, and for the second time that day, she cried.

Epilogue

ONE YEAR LATER

Gladys sat on a portable folding chair in a graveyard, staring at Roy's gravestone absentmindedly until little drops of rain woke her up and brought her back to the present.

"Hi, big boy, been a whole year already. Still haven't changed the bed. Still haven't canceled all your stupid fishing magazines. And I still haven't canceled that football channel package you got for the cable. Can't believe that the one chivalrous thing you did for me had to put you in the ground. Most of the money I found in your old golf bag is gone. Going to have to make it last, or I'm going to need to find a real job next spring. Are you cold up there? I'm cold. It's getting cold," Gladys said almost in a whisper. Beebee barked as if to say hi to her master's dead husband.

"much familiar. champion. wow!" thought Beebee.

"What's with you?" Gladys asked Beebee. "So, Roy, I still see the momma-thon roll past, and some of the babies have turned into little walking brats already. Pretty soon they're gonna be old enough to ask for candy on Halloween. Don't think I'll make a convincing Bigfoot monster like you did," Gladys resumed, ignoring Beebee. But

Beebee insisted to taking on part in the conversation and gave another loud bark.

"Right. It's not a monster, it's just big. Hey, Roy, apparently Beebee has learned English. Or you possessed her. Anyway, shit, it's starting to rain. I just wanted to wish you a happy death anniversary and give you some flowers," Gladys added.

She laid the flowers on his gravestone and stared at it some more. Her mind was too full with random thoughts and torturous memories that it all seemed fuzzy and blurred. Beebee kept barking persistently.

"What?!?" Gladys asked in annoyance. Beebee ran off without another bark, towards the nearby woods. "Come back! What the hell are you doing?!? Beebee! Beebee, come! Come!"

Past the edge of the cemetery, through some brush in an adjacent park, Beebee ran to a small creek in the woods. She kept barking, calling for Gladys to follow. Gladys was far behind her, but she was catching up. When she finally reached the creek, she saw Beebee sitting and wagging her tail. She was nose to nose with old Charlemagne! He was very skinny, and his ribs were protruding from the sides of his body. There were scruff marks and some past injuries that had never healed poking through bald spots in his fur. He looked like the past year had been very, very hard on him.

"much survivor. champion. very brave. wow," barked Beebee.

"Charlemagne! Poor baby, what happened to you! Come here," Gladys murmured, as she squatted to pat old Charlemagne. He limped slowly towards Gladys. Gladys tickled him behind the ears, and her fingers got caught on his collar. She held Charlemagne's head steady so she could look at it. It said his was name Boris. As she was trying to read the rest of it, she didn't notice the tall, handsome man across the creek. He was wearing a crisp white shirt and jeans. He had a great head of hair that matched the color of Charlemagne.

"Jesus Christ! Damn you. Damn you, old age," Harry muttered, as he grabbed a tree for support while he tried to catch his breath. "I can't run after doggies like I used to. Come here Boris!" Finally, he straightened up, catching Gladys's amused and curious eyes. "Oh wow, you made a friend, I see. Hi, I'm Harry," Harry said, his face turning red with an embarrassment he wasn't embarrassed to show.

"Hi, I'm Gladys. Nice to meet you. My dog came running too. They must have smelled each other from far away," Gladys replied, as she stood up and grabbed Beebee's leash.

"You know my dog?" Harry asked in

surprise.

"Yes. I've seen him before. I mean, I know him well. I've seen him many times," Gladys replied, her voice trailing with every revision. "Hey, what the fuck happened to him?" she managed to ask.

"My dog Blitz, he passed away. So I went to the pound and found Boris here. He was in the last holding pen. He looked so scared and sick and skinny. I wanted to take care of him. I just got him this week. He must have been in the woods for a long time, fending for himself," Harry explained affectionately.

"Yes, about a year," Gladys replied absentmindedly. "How do you know?" Harry asked.

"Um, Harry. It's a long story. Long and nutso. You don't want to know. But I will say, the only innocent one in the sad affair was this guy. Who, by the way, is not named Boris. His name is Charlemagne. I know the world gives you the right to name him what you want. But please! Boris? Really? He's not a ferret. That's a ferret name," Gladys replied, her voice jumping from dismissive and indifferent to annoyed and indignant.

"It was my father's name," Harry replied solemnly.

"Oh. Crap. Sorry," Gladys replied, trying for

sincerity. She just couldn't help it, and a small laugh escaped her lips. "Sorry."

"It's cool. Thanks for finding my dog. And I'll think about the name," Harry replied. Harry attached the leash to Charlemagne's collar and walked away, but Charlemagne wouldn't budge. He pulled back towards Beebee. Beebee acknowledged him with a bark. "Come on, dude!" Harry begged Charlemagne.

"Wait," Gladys said as she knelt down and removed Beebee's leash, "Try this."

"What are you doing?"

After unhooking Beebee's leash, Gladys leaned forward and unhooked Charlemagne's before standing up. She brushed the dirt off her knees as she watched the dogs circle each other, smelling each other's privates. Then Charlemagne made a face that could almost be called a grin before mounting Beebee, like they'd done a little over a year ago.

"Oh my God," Harry blurted out in amazement.

"Motherfucking right. There you go, kids. Get it in," Gladys murmured proudly.

"You can't be serious. You're like a doggy pimp!" Harry indignantly said, but he couldn't help but laugh.

"Yeah, she's my bitch," Gladys admitted jokingly. "Hey, how often do you come here?" "Every day... almost," Harry replied distractedly, as he watched the dogs copulate. "Ever come at night?" Gladys asked. "Night walking in the woods? That's..."

"Insane?" Gladys finished for him. "Yeah, and? Come by tomorrow."

"Will you be here?" Harry asked, his eyes gleaming with mischief and friendliness. "Sure. Beebee, too," Gladys replied, and turned her attention back to the reunited couple just in time. "What the fuck?!?" Harry exclaimed, as he saw Charlemagne's most guarded secret. "Third penis!"

THE END

www.ingramcontent.com/pod-product-compliance
Lightning Source LLC
Chambersburg PA
CBHW030541130626
46552CB00006B/2363